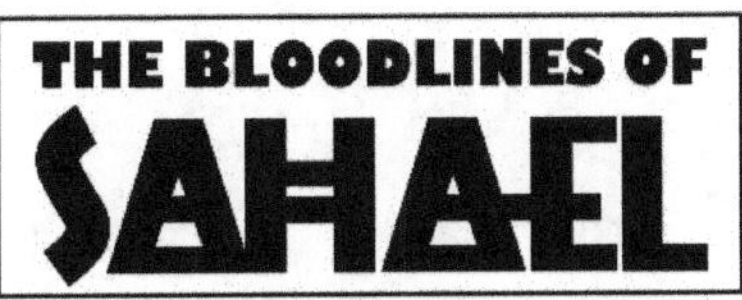

THE BLOODLINES OF SAHAEL

VOLUME TWO

BOOK TWO

THE THIRD SIGN

BY

DWAYNE ANTHONY MADRY

Printed in the United States of America

First Printing, 2024

Cover Design by JessHavok

ISBN 978-1-963089-37-0

www.SAHAEL.com

Intoduction into Sahael

Aamira had escaped the clutches of her past, crossing the treacherous Nambian Strait and setting her sights on the enigmatic desert Sandlands of IFF. Each grain of sand beneath her feet whispered secrets of a world steeped in ancient power and unfathomable mystery. As she journeyed through this arid expanse, a fateful encounter awaited her—a solitary man, a guardian of wisdom bound to the very essence of Aarde.

In their presence, a profound connection sparked, an awakening that resonated through the land itself. Suddenly, the earth began to tremble, a harbinger of the Third Sign, a portent of the cataclysmic forces stirring beneath the surface. Aamira felt the pulse of the planet, a rhythmic thrum that matched the racing of her heart. The ground quaked and shifted, a chaotic dance that signaled the impending upheaval. Mountains groaned as if waking from a deep slumber, their majestic forms succumbing to the relentless forces of nature. Cities, once vibrant and full of life, began to collapse under the weight of their own histories, the very foundations crumbling as the land writhed in turmoil.

Yet, even as the world around her descended into chaos, a fierce resolve ignited within her soul. This was not merely an escape; it was a reckoning. The sacred blood flowing through her veins intertwined her fate with that of Aarde, and she felt the call of destiny urging her onward. The earthquakes were not just a sign of destruction; they were a clarion call, a reminder that she was part of something far greater than herself.

Navigating through the tumult, Aamira pressed forward, her heart set on reaching SAHAEL—the fabled sanctuary whispered of in legends, where safety and wisdom awaited those brave enough to seek it. The winds howled around her, carrying the echoes of lost souls and forgotten dreams, yet she remained undeterred.

In the heart of the storm, Aamira would discover her true strength. With each tremor beneath her feet, she embraced her role as a beacon of hope, a harbinger of change in a world teetering on the brink of annihilation. As the Third Sign unfolded, she understood that her journey was not just about survival; it was about forging her legacy amidst the chaos, where the extraordinary awaited those willing to confront the tempest head-on.

And so, as the earth roared and the skies darkened, Aamira set her sights on SAHAEL, ready to confront the trials that lay ahead, determined to rise and etch her name into the annals of history, where legends are born and destinies are fulfilled.

CHAPTER CONTENTS

CHAPTER I
YORUBAN HISTORY

The Desert Sand Lands of IFF, Karnak Temple

Aamira had never felt such heat. The sun blazed down as her feet pressed into the coarse sand. Lips parched, limbs tired, she followed Abioye and his assassin friend Adewara toward the city of Beth-din. Dunes stretched off into the distance with no sign of inhabitants anywhere.

For two hours they had braved the open desert. The weakened slaves behind them stumbled along. They had barely escaped captivity the day before. Would they die free less than 48 hours after their liberation?

The anger Aamira had felt ebbed as her dry tongue scraped against the roof of her mouth. After seeing the murdered slave encampment that morning, she had wanted to slaughter every witan she encountered. Her blossoming abilities had given her a confidence that had been foreign to her. Now though, all she wanted was water. She would trade vengeance for a cold sip of tea or a bite of a ripe orange.

Occasionally the entourage would pass through a grove of Marula trees, encountering large camel spiders the size of rats that could run up to 15 miles per hour. Adewara killed two of them as the creatures rushed from behind trees to attack the tired slaves trudging along behind the leaders.

"Watch your feet and legs," Abioye said to Aamira, pointing toward a Marula tree that had thick spider webs wrapped around the trunk. "Camel spiders aren't the only arachnid to worry about out here. Wind spiders can fly and attack you in the air when caught in the current of wind. Sun spiders are nasty too. They appear out of small sand deposits of quicksand when the sun is hottest."

"I don't see any more of them," Aamira said as she started to rub her arms nervously.

Abioye nodded. "I can hear and feel them beneath my feet as they sift under the sand. The wind spiders are altering the air currents; we need to be careful. The temperature is also increasing the likelihood of the sun spiders coming to the surface to eat and see us as the food. We need to hurry."

The mysterious Abioye seemed to know so much about this land. Aamira had met him by chance weeks before during the plantation riots. He hadn't wanted her to join their group escaping to the Sand Lands of IFF. His gruffness hadn't changed, even when Aamira's powers manifested, and she shook the earth or formed blades of green energy from her hands. He continued to keep secrets, particularly about his family. Now, according to the Hashashin assassin Adewara, Abioye was the prince of this land. What kind of kingdom could exist out here? And why would Abioye keep it a secret?

Several more camel spiders scurried from the sand and rushed at an old woman leaning against a dry Marula trunk. Adewara leaped forward with a dagger and cut two of them in half before impaling the third and holding it up for everyone to see.

"These flesh-eating spiders numb you with their bite and then start to eat chunks of flesh out of your body," he shouted so all could hear. "You won't even realize it until it's too late.

Respect this land by being cautious at all times. I can't be everywhere to protect you."

They continued on, passing another cluster of trees, when a scream from the back of the caravan drew Aamira's attention.

"More spiders!" Adewara shouted as he yanked his dagger from his belt and started running. Aamira and Abioye followed.

More cries.

Near the back of the group, dozens of spiders swarmed a group of young girls. They jumped around frantically as spiders crawled on their legs and feet.

"One of them stepped on a hive!" Abioye yelled. He picked up a large stick and started knocking away the sun spiders from the girls. Aamira stepped on some of them, leaving crunching sounds behind.

There were too many spiders. More crawled out of the sand, larger, with bright yellow markings on their thorax.

"Sun spiders!" Adewara cried. "Get back! Get back now!"

Aamira's bracelet started to light up and emanate as the camel and sun spiders crawled up her legs. She instinctively conjured a Yoruban Bo glaive staff with sharp blades at each end.

She swung her weapon, slicing the camel spiders in two as they oozed over the sand.

"Look!" Abioye shouted, pointing to the tree limbs above. A gust of wind drove dozens of other spiders toward them, swinging from strands of web as if flying. The freed slaves shrieking in terror.

"Wind spiders! Cut them down! Cut them down!" Adewara cried.

Aamira used her Yoruban glaive to attack the wind spiders as they swung toward a grouping of elderly followers. Abioye helped by knocking them out of the sky. The sun spiders began consuming the dead bodies of their slain compatriots.

"Kill more of them!" Aamira yelled. "They're eating their dead. That will draw them away from us."

Bloodlust returned to Aamira's heart as she stabbed at spiders, pinning them to the bark of the nearest tree. Each stroke of her staff led to the death of a creature, and Aamira imagined each arachnid as being a witan slaver, crying out for mercy.

She screamed and slashed, kicking up sand with every movement.

"It's okay," Abioye said, grabbing her staff. "They're all dead."

Aamira stood there for a moment, sweat dripping from her nose. Her chest heaved and she looked around. She hadn't merely killed the spiders; she had dismembered them brutally.

"That is a warrior right there," Adewara smiled as he wiped at his brow. "You must have been trained since childhood."

"…You'd think," Abioye said after a pause.

As they finished helping the group of girls, Adewara, Abioye, and Aamira took a minute to catch their breath.

"Are you okay?" Aamira asked one of the girls as perspiration dripped from her face.

"We're okay. Thank you for saving our lives," the girls said as they quickly ran back to the other freed slaves.

"That was close," Abioye said, sheathing his knife. "Let's continue. We have many more miles in the open desert."

"We need water," Aamira said as her staff faded and disappeared.

Adewara reached up and plucked a leaf from one of the few

Marula trees in the cluster. He tossed the leaf in his mouth and started to chew.

"Have everyone take a few leaves from the trees here," he said, pointing to the group. "Chew them slowly. It will help with dehydration and provide respite from the parch that comes with desert travel. Once the leaf becomes chalky in your mouth after about a half hour, spit it out. Let's go."

After two more hours of crossing the desert, and Aamira spitting out three leaves once they became too bitter to bear, the enclave arrived on the edge of a cliff that looked down on a river a thousand feet below.

"We must climb down and cross," Adewara said as a breeze blew his scarf over his shoulder. He turned to the gathering of exhausted people, dark skin glistening in the sun. "This will be the most dangerous part of our journey, so be ready! This river runs to the coast. The canyon opens up a few miles from here and witans have taken the beachhead. We've encountered many naval vessels making their way north along the currents. General Scipio of the Narsan and the Ennead forces have sent soldiers this way for the past few months. We very likely will encounter witan forces as we try to cross. Be wary! Stay close together."

Soon Adewara was leading them down a path that cut into the cliff. The air was cooler once they entered the shadow of the canyon. Aamira could smell the moisture. She wanted to leap from the path and dive deep into the river, to drink and be satisfied.

"I sense you're eager for a fight," Abioye said as they trudged down the zig-zagging path. "You seem different than you did all those weeks ago as we escaped the burning plantations."

"And you're the same," Aamira replied as she helped steady an old woman stumbling along behind her. "You're secretive."

Abioye remained silent.

They reached the banks of the river. The roar of the water echoed through the canyon ominously. Aamira stopped to rest and splash her face. The water revived her spirits and tasted sweet after the bitterness of the leaves. For a moment, everyone seemed to feel at peace as they drank.

In a cove to their right sat a collection of wooden boats with oars.

"These Hashashin longboats are log canoes we can take to the other side of the lake," Adewara said as he pointed at the craft. We have no time to wait. You can rest on our way to the other side."

The people paddled weakly across the river. There weren't enough boats for so many people, but after several trips there and back, everyone stood on the far side.

Abioye looked up toward the cliff face a thousand feet high in front of them. "We need to head up the path and escape the canyon. If a patrol comes by, we will be easy targets. Let's go!"

The group began trudging up the winding path one by one. Aamira stayed near the back with Adewara and Abioye to make sure the people made it out safely.

A horn blew from somewhere down the canyon, barely registering above the river's growl.

"Run, now!" Adewara cried.

In a panic, the people began clamoring up the path toward the upper lip of the canyon.

"What's going on? Aamira asked.

"Look!" Abioye said, pointing behind them.

Several long boats came into view around the river bend full of witan naval soldiers, bows and arrows at the ready.

"Go! Go! Go!" Aamira shouted, leaping up the path and pushing people to move faster.

Several naval militiamen fired. Arrows struck two people at the back of the group. They fell with cries of pain and rolled back down the path. Another volley of arrows flew. One hit Aamira in the hip area.

"Aamira!" Abioye cried.

Pain seared in Aamira's leg. She held to the rock wall to keep from falling as several more freed slaves tumbled to the water below. Aamira's eyes immediately turned dark green as tattoos started to appear all over her body. She dropped to her knees, as a green aura covered her body. The arrow popped from her leg as if pushed out from the inside.

Pebbles pressed against her hands as she crouched there, hearing the screams of terrified people.

Witans must die, she thought. *They must all die.*

The land beneath her palms started to tremble and quake. Aamira felt all of Aarde beneath her. She felt each rock and clump of dirt. She felt the water rushing over boulders the size of houses.

A shockwave erupted from the path where Aamira crouched. Chunks of rock shot up from beneath the river, smashing into the longboats and splintering them. Soldiers flew into the air and crashed down to the water before disappearing beneath the surface. The ground started to shift and tremble, creating untold amounts of destruction everywhere.

"Stop!" Adewara yelled.

Aamira opened her eyes and saw that the path was beginning to crack and pull away from the cliff wall. She stood, and the earthquake instantly stopped.

"What was that? What are you?" Abioye asked, staring at

Aamira's fierce emerald eyes.

"I am that I am," Aamira answered.

"Meaning what?" Abioye asked.

"I am the Black Madonna of the Yoruban bloodline," Aamira said.

Abioye just looked at Aamira. He blinked several times.

"What Solomon has said is true!" Adewara shouted, smile broad. "You're the last of an ancient bloodline that was thought eradicated by Lord Commander Natas after the Narsans infiltrated Sahael and destroyed the Quad-cities. That led to the Ennead destroying Khartoum Palace, bringing it down to never rise again."

"That's what I've been told," Aamira said.

"Die tekens van die tyd is op hande," Adewara said in the Sahaelian tongue.

"I've heard that before," Aamira said. "Solomon said it on several occasions. He told me the Educators speak like that. Are you an Educator?"

"I am," Adewara nodded. "I was trained in Timbuktu and act as counselor and teacher in the courts of Beth-din."

"You know about the bloodlines and Solomon's plans," Aamira stated, suddenly excited. "You can teach me things I never knew to ask Solomon when I had the chance."

Adewara looked at the people staring scared at Aamira. "Perhaps later. Now is not the time. These people are startled and tired."

"I'm aware," Aamira nodded, dusting the dirt from her hands. "Let's get out of the canyon. We can talk more along the journey.

The group reached the sand above and Adewara continued

leading the group into the desert. Abioye stood close by but continued his silence.

"You are a Black Madonna," Adewara grinned as they trudged through the sand. "We've been waiting for news of your existence. Some had doubted the prophecies."

"Solomon has spoken with me and my sisters," Aamira said. "Explaining that I needed to get to the Desert Sand Lands of IFF. Solomon didn't explain why it was essential to discovering my true purpose. This is why I asked for your help. Will you help me find that purpose?"

"Yes, it's imperative that we get you to Beth-din as soon as possible," Adewara said. He looked at Abioye. "Do you agree, my prince?"

"The Signs of the Times are upon us," Abioye answered.

Aamira kicked at the sand, paying close attention to how each granule seemed to call out to her, giving its allegiance to her every command.

"I have heard about the signs of the times," she said. "Solomon told me they would soon fall upon all of Aarde. When he spoke to my sisters and I inside of his tent after the Royal Rumble, almost four months ago, he said many things that seemed impossible to me. I'll admit, I wasn't a very good student to his lessons. I had grown accustomed to my comfortable life. Now I long to fight like I never have before. I want vengeance."

Adewara nodded. "Such was it foretold. The Signs of the Times are indicated and are to be brought back to Aarde by the sacred bloodlines; those who are not lost but are hidden and require an awakening. The signs are for the remnants to know that hope is here and that they can fight for their freedom and their right to survive returning to Sahael. These are those who have been taken away and dispersed from their lands over four hundred years ago, long before the fall of Sahael. The awakening has started to take place; the events happening around you at this moment are not coincidence. You will lead your people."

"My people?" Aamira asked as she rubbed sweat from her neck.

"Yes!" Adewara said, motioning to the tired group stumbling across the dunes. "They're your people, and they need saving. And not just these wretched souls here. Millions more throughout Aarde. After seeing you touch the lands with your feet and see Aarde shift under you, I know the times are here. You need to learn about your people. The witans have kept your bloodline in the dark. Learning about all your people and your history is pertinent. Once you've learned what's needed, everything suddenly will start to flow through your mind about your people."

"Your people?" Abioye said as he looked at Aamira. His face was a calm mask.

Adewara stopped and nodded. "Yes. Her people."

Aamira didn't know how to act around Abioye at that moment. If he was a prince, did he fear losing his power? Would he become her enemy if she tried to follow Solomon's will? She dared not deny what she was any longer. For far too long Aamira had taken a back seat. No more. She was ready to lead…she just didn't know how to do it.

"Then we may be of the same blood, however distantly," Abioye said.

"That's not correct, you were adopted into the Yoruban bloodline for your own safety," Adewara said as they continued leading the group through the desert.

"What more can you tell me about these signs that have been set in motion?" Aamira asked. "You seem to know a lot more than I do. I know Solomon told me many things, but I was too stupid to listen."

"Let's continue to Beth-din and I can explain on the way," Adewara said. "We need to hurry before all of the hidden spiders come above land to see us as their next meal. They are growing restless. I can see the subtle signs. As the ground beneath us continues to shake with our footsteps, they'll become more restless. Their homes from below are unstable, forcing them to the surface."

"This is why we need to get Beth-din," Abioye said.

Adewara nodded, crossing his arms. "Indeed, they will look to the cities next. The spider population has exploded over the past few years. The sooner we get to Beth-din, the better."

The sun burned high in the sky above. The dunes went on forever in all directions, punctuated by the occasional Marula grove. Adewara gave Aamira a scarf to cover her face and shield her head from the sun.

"I'm excited you're here, Aamira of Sahael," he smiled. "We were told of your coming. Many of the wealthy class did not believe it, but Educators like me are patient and trusting."

"How did you know I would come?" Aamira asked.

"Years ago, Solomon the protector of Aarde approached me about a virgin, a black Madonna in Vannadale of the sacred bloodline," Adewara began. "Solomon explained that you would be escaping, restoring the hopes of your people who are of the sacred blood. Lord Commander Natas wants to see the sacred blood destroyed, so getting to you before your powers manifested was paramount, He hasn't stopped hunting you and your cousins since the fall of Sahael."

Aamira's eyes widened. "This would have been before the Royal Rumble when I met Solomon?"

"Yes. Solomon is playing a game that spans centuries. He

isn't all-knowing, but he reads the patterns of men and sees what is potentially coming long before it happens. He knew Natas would become the grand threat and did his best to stop it. When that failed, he did his best to restore our people. After speaking with Solomon, the protector of Aarde, Abioye's mother and father sanctioned the rebellions that were designed to smuggle the princesses out of Vannadale with one of our Educators on the inside. Things did not go according to plan, but by the grave of Ishtar and Obatala, you and Abioye met, and now you're here."

Aamira looked over her shoulder at the prince as he trudged behind them next to a group of elderly women, oblivious to their conversation. "If Abioye had his way, he would have left me behind."

"Abioye was never privy to all the plans running concurrently," Adewara replied. "He had his assassination mission, which he failed. I believe his anger and shame have clouded his mind."

"My sisters and I always talked about leaving the estates," Aamira said. "I never really wanted to. I was too comfortable."

"Comfort can be dangerous," Adewara said, looking down at the sand as they walked. "It is a trap too many people, both Sahaelian and witan, fall into. Comfort is an illusion."

After a few more hours, the group crested a dune and looked down on the city of Beth-din. Yellow buildings of sandstone blended into the desert, making it difficult for Aamira to tell exactly how big the city was.

"We've reached the city of Beth-din," Adewara said. "This stretch of the Iffian desert is dotted with quicksand traps, sandstorms, and sand rain. With so many refugees with us, it is best all of you stay here. I'll cross the dune and enter the city alone, bringing back supplies and a plan for what to do next."

"Find out what my mother and father would have us do," Abioye said. "I will stay here until ordered otherwise."

"Good idea, we'll just wait outside the city," Aamira said.

"Okay, I'll be right back," Adewara said.

Adewara didn't return until sunset. He arrived with a dozen other men dressed in similar robes and face-covering scarfs. They carried backpacks and water skins. The people shouted for joy, some of them falling to the sand and praising Ishtar when they took their first drink of water since the river earlier that afternoon.

"We need to hurry," Adewara said to Abioye and Aamira. "There's a storm coming in. We need to hurry if we want to beat it."

"Let's get to the city," Aamira said, stepping toward Bethdin.

"We are not going to the city, Aamira," Adewara warned.

"Where are we going now?" Aamira asked, rolling her eyes.

"The Temple of Karnak to meet up with Abioye's mother and father; King and Queen Adesola," Adewara replied.

"What about destroying Abingdale's trafficking trade?" Aamira asked. "What about getting the refugees safe to the city?"

"We have more important matters that need our attention at the moment," Adewara said, with a somber tone in his voice. "And as for the people you brought with you; they will be taken into the city under cover of darkness. They will be cared for. It will only be myself, Prince Abioye, and you, Aamira, who will be going to Karnak." He turned to Abioye. "Prince Abioye, your mother and father weren't in the city, but they left me a message about heading to Karnak as soon as possible. It appears enemies from within have started attacking Beth-din, forcing the King and Queen to take refuge in Karnak."

"Who would betray the crown?" Abioye asked, muscles suddenly tight.

Adewara shook his head and looked at the first stars blinking in the darkening sky. "You know of our divisions. We haven't been united in a generation."

"Is it a civil war?" Aamira asked. She had assumed the desert people would be more unified and ready to fight against the witan oppressors in the outer lands. Why else would Solomon have sent her here? A divided people would be no help in freeing Sahaelian slaves if they were too busy fighting among themselves.

"We can discuss all of this along the way." Adewara whistled loudly suddenly. The men in his entourage did the same, including Abioye, until a note so high-pitched was achieved that it shook Aamira's teeth.

The sand at their feet vibrated until what looked like a large, hairy pink worm the size of a horse emerged from the dune, followed by two others.

"These sandworms will move us across the desert at a good pace," Adewara said. "Climb on and hold to the hairs, Aamira. They will follow their paths in the dark and take us to Karnak."

"What is Karnak?" Abioye asked as he straddled one of the worms. Aamira did the same. She expected the creature to be slimy, but its skin was coarse with thick and tangled hair.

Adewara whistled again and the worms lurched forward. The sand rushed by, sounding more like the ocean than a dry desert.

"Adewara," Abioye shouted over the air blowing past them as they rode. "What is Karnak? I've never heard of this place."

"It was agreed upon that if the foundations of the Aarde started to shake, all remaining Yorubans were to convene at Karnak. No exceptions," Adewara answered.

"Why are the foundations of Aarde shaking?" Aamira asked.

"Because you are literally shaking them," Adewara shouted as the worms kicked up sand directly into their faces as they drove down the nearest dune. "I felt it today in the canyon. Abioye told me you did it before too when all of you were escaping the plantations."

"This is all because of me?" Aamira said. "How would anyone have known about me shaking the ground with my abilities? Why would they gather in this Karnak place if they didn't know about me even coming here to IFF?"

"There have been other signs," Adewara said. "This decision to go to Karnak was made many years ago when you were spotted in the city of Venn, and many in Vannadale started speaking of a young girl with green eyes among the enslaved community. Many wanted to purchase you and make you a wife or a breeder to prop up as a means to help control other women and the enslaved population in Vannadale." Adewara said.

"I have so many questions about my people and the sacred bloodlines. I'd like to know more," Aamira said. She had opportunities to learn from Solomon, and she had squandered them. She would listen now and possibly learn things she should have known already.

"I can tell you what I know," Adewara replied. "Before the Invasion of Sahael, the Ancient Anunnaki and the Chosen

Negrunde bloodlines merged, creating the Yoruban bloodline. The Sacred bloodlines never had the opportunity to take their authentic places in Sahael, even after everyone had left."

"The Anunnaki and the Negrunde? Those are new names to me," Aamira said.

"When Sahael and the Quad-Cities were destroyed, the people that remained alive of the sacred bloodlines were placed in airships by the Narsans. Lord Commander Natas sought to splice the bloodlines, sending half of the Yorubans to the provinces and the other half to the outer lands, to be systematically controlled by the witans.

"The fact these Yorubans are still alive is a testament to their will, strength, and resolve," Aamira said, hanging onto every word coming out of Adewara's mouth.

Adewara smiled. "Ancient Kemetic magic was used to protect the four bloodlines by Kaimana and Kanoa, who gave the leaders of the four bloodlines the ability to save their posterity by masking their eyes. This made the princesses look like normal Alkebulans, thus saving them from eradication. It allowed them to be placed on enslavement ships, shackled, bound, and shipped to the outer lands and the provinces."

"It's a miracle they survived at all," Aamira said.

"Lord Commander Natas saw no use for them after seeing they all had brown eyes. So, he sent them to the outer lands after Khartoum palace was destroyed by the Narsans. The sacred bloodlines were rumored to have been killed; while the rest of the Sahaelians were scattered all over Aarde."

"Living in a world where witans think they're the majority is a scary thought. Don't they know that they're the minority?" Aamira asked.

Abioye shook his head and spoke for the first time since

setting out on the worms. "They flipped the script…the narrative. They perceive their superiority through their own ignorance…not that our people have done much to prove them wrong over the past twenty years."

Aamira couldn't deny that Abioye spoke the truth. Still, true or not, his words made her angry. His demeanor made her angry. Did she hate Abioye? If not, she was as close to it as a person could be.

"What happened to my people after the ships?" Aamira asked, ignoring Abioye's commentary.

"They were sent to the inner provinces to be used as slaves to help boost colonial economies," Adewara continued. "They are worked almost to death until they are no longer useful to their enslavers and then placed on boats to arrive here in the Sand Lands of IFF to be used for sport and hunting by wealthy patrons. It's disgusting."

Aamira closed her eyes as sand blew in her face. She had seen the suffering on the ships firsthand. She had seen the old and withered men and women. To think they would have been hunted like animals while witan men and women stood smiling over their dead bodies like they would a deer, made her sick.

Her anger grew unchecked, as it had steadily since she had killed the men on the boat.

The wind blew harder, and Aamira found it almost impossible to open her eyes because of the flying sand all around her.

"The storm has caught us from the south," Adewara shouted. "We need to stop and set up shelter until it passes. We'll stay here for the rest of the night."

Adewara took out his backpack and unfurled a canvas tent. In mere moments, he and Abioye had a shelter in place. The three entered just as the wind howled all the louder, spitting up dust that choked the air and would suffocate anyone caught in the tempest.

The worms slithered beneath the surface and disappeared.

CHAPTER II
IRREVERSIBLE EVENTS

The Desert Sand Lands of IFF, Karnak Temple

Aamira, Abioye, and Adewara sat inside of the spacious tent as the sandstorm passed. Wind pelted the canvas while they sat in the light of a single candle.

Adewara had pulled out a book and flipped through the pages. He told Aamira it was a Nalice Journal, magically linked to the library at Timbuktu, where he could search all knowledge available to the Educator class.

"Now that we've some time to rest until this storm passes," Adewara spoke, "there's another urgent matter that needs to be discussed about events centered around Aarde itself that have recently taken place. I learned in a brief visit to Beth-din earlier this afternoon that General Scipio is planning an operation called *Red Dog* designed to hunt down all of Aamira's people and destroy them. The Signs of the times are forcing the Yorubans to Karnak or be eradicated if they choose to stay in their current areas."

Aamira was shocked. "How could they possibly all be hunted down? Even all the witan armies joined together couldn't slaughter so many people."

"The Yorubans are not united," Adewara said as he turned a page in the journal. "None of the bloodlines has coalesced behind a leader. We're all scattered and weak. Natas has vision and determination. Of all the bloodlines, the Yorubans are the most known to him. He knows their population centers in the wider world. Their threat is gravest of all now that the signs are manifesting. Natas is not blind to such things. Yorubans will have to choose death in the cities or life in the sanctuary, before the order is given. Scipio and Natas are patient. They've proven to be willing to wait years…decades even, for the right moment to strike."

"This is all happening because of me, the moment I stepped foot on this land; I doomed many of my people," Aamira said.

Adewara shrugged. "I don't know, but all Yorubans are returning to Karnak. The order won't be issued in time for some. Many will make it. Many won't. The traitors in Beth-din will likely be slaughtered."

"With all of the Yorubans returning, they can be followed, exposing its location," Abioye said.

"Karnak is hidden and will keep the people from revealing our location." Adewara looked at Aamira. "I feel your presence here has set events in motion that we don't fully understand yet."

"This is all so confusing," Aamira said.

"In time, you will come to understand what is happening. This is a lot for you to take in. The Signs of The Times are upon us with different interpretations of what they are and how they cover the lands. Rumors of quakes are spreading from all over Aarde."

"But I've only shaken the ground twice with my powers. "I didn't even know I could do it. Solomon was always vague about what I could do, saying only that I would know what to do on instinct."

"I don't think the quakes are your doing specifically," Adewara breathed. "They are part of a grander change. I've heard whispers in the past weeks about shifts in ocean currents as well, even air currents too. The change to Aarde is immense, but it is tied to the princesses and the redemption of Sahael. Of that I have no doubt."

The Sandstorm grew increasingly worse, blowing the top of the tent away with a booming force.

"Cover your eyes!" Abioye cried.

Adewara scrambled to grab his books and supplies. Aamira pulled a scarf over her face and hugged the sand. Tiny grains pelted her body, scouring her skin.

For hours they lay silent, letting the storm pass.

By morning, the sky had cleared. Aamira sat up, spilling almost an inch of sand from her body. She was tired and dirty; thirsty and hungry.

"Are you both alright?" Adewara asked.

"I haven't seen a storm like that in a couple years," Abioye said as he dusted sand from his clothes.

"Eat and drink quickly," Adewara said, handing a leather sack of dried fruit and a water bag to Aamira. "We need to maneuver through this sand carefully or we'll get lost and find ourselves in a different part of this desert."

Adewara tried calling for sandworms several times with his high-pitched whistle, but no creatures responded. They started walking instead, but after two hours their path was impeded.

"By Ishtar," Adewara whispered as they crested a dune.

Below them in a small desert valley camped a military force with at least a thousand men dressed in the blue and red garb of General Scipio's army.

"We are in Gore. Find somewhere to hide," Adewara said.

"Gore?" Aamira asked as they ran down the back side of the dune.

"Gore is a mobile stronghold controlled by General Scipio's," Abioye said.

"The prince is right," Adewara confirmed. "Their whole purpose is to keep track of every Yoruban in IFF, preventing them from entering the area where they believe Karnak to be. They are constantly patrolling the Karnak Sand Seas, as they call them. I had no idea they had mobilized so many troops in the area. The last time I was here, they had two dozen soldiers for the entire area. This is unexpected."

"I wonder how my parents got past them," Abioye said.

Adewara pointed to the northern side of the dune, "Let's do some reconnaissance and see what we can see."

They crouched along the sand until they came to a lower lip and could gaze over the edge at the military force.

"See there," Adewara said, pointing at what looked like a line of dead bodies in the sand. "There was a battle near here. The army lost a good number of men."

"I don't see any Sahaelian bodies among the dead," Abioye whispered.

"Scipio's soldiers would be no match at all for your parents and the elite guard," Adewara smiled. "I'm sure they retreated quickly after suffering severe losses. I would guess your parents made it to Karnak safely after that."

"What about us?" Aamira asked. "Three against a thousand? I don't think we're going to have the same success rate."

Abioye pushed himself from the sand as if to stand. "I don't care about the odds. I need to find my parents. They may need my help."

"No, stay here. Let's be patient," Adewara said as he pulled on Abioye's shirt sleeve.

"We need to find his parents," Aamira said.

"Soon your people will be trying to get within the walls of Karnak," Adewara continued, "but there is a Nairo Gate that is operational, so they hide awaiting safe entry until they are summoned to come home."

"What's beyond the Nairo Gate?" Aamira said.

"We need to get out of here and get to Karnak as quickly as possible," Adewara said, not answering Aamira's question.

"We need a plan for getting across undetected," Abioye added.

"We wait and travel under the cover of darkness," Adewara suggested. "Let us cover ourselves with what remains of the tent. Try to sleep as best you can through the heat of the day. Tonight, we cross."

Under cover of darkness, Adewara, Abioye, and Aamira snuck around the valley. Night became their ally, making it difficult for them to be spotted by General Scipio's scouts. As they rounded the dune, they came upon three witan soldiers urinating in the sand.

"Now is our chance," Abioye whispered from behind a rock. "They're vulnerable. We can kill all three and move on."

Aamira smiled. The thought of killing these men appealed

to her. She manifested a green blade in her right hand, but Adewara placed his hand on her wrist to constrain her.

"If we kill these men needlessly, it will alert the army to our presence. I know you both are angry and want vengeance, but this is not a good plan."

Abioye nodded, though his eyes stared fixed at the three men as they laughed and wandered back toward the camp.

As the night grew older, the trio walked in silence. Aamira wondered what it would have felt like to kill those men, to feel their blood on her hands and watch the life drain from them. Would it have made her happy? Did she even care about that anymore?

As the sun rose, Adewara led them into a small canyon that looked unimportant and mostly concealed by the greater dunes.

"This is the entrance to Karnak," he said. "Stay close."

Inside the canyon, footprints covered the sand. The sheltered nature of the crevasse kept the wind from obliterating them as it had in the outer sands.

After an hour in the confines of the canyon, the gorge ended at a cliff face with sandstone doors carved onto the rock. The image of a Marula tree filled the center of the doors, along with carvings running up the sides that looked similar to the tattoos that would glow on Aamira's skin when she used her powers.

"Is this Karnak?" Aamira asked.

"No." Adewara shook his head. "These are the Nairo Gates I spoke of."

"We need to get past the Nairo Gate and gain entry into Karnak," Abioye said. "I need to know if my parents survived General Scipio's soldiers."

As Aamira looked at the doors, several hundred people

crept out from caves hidden in the walls. They wore pale colored desert garb with scarfs protecting their dark skin from the harsh sun and sand. Thousands of Yoruban men, women, and children, suddenly stood up from the sand where they had been hiding using sandbanks to keep their whereabouts secret.

"Where did they come from?" Abioye said, stepping back.

"There's so many of them!" Aamira gasped.

"They can't get in," Adewara replied. "They've been waiting for someone to open the doors."

"Why can't they get in?" Aamira asked. "They're of the Yoruban bloodline, right? Otherwise, they wouldn't know to come here."

Adewara waved to the people to come closer. "They need someone of royal blood to open the gate. Gather, all of you! You are safe!"

"No one can get in?" Abioye spat. "Why set up a retreat plan like this if no one can open the damn doors? I was always taught to trust Educators, but this is foolish in the extreme!"

Adewara looked at Aamira. "Someone can open the gate, that is certain, and the reason they've gathered here is because they still have faith in Ishtar and Obatala. They have faith in the promise of a reunited Sahael."

"These people are waiting on me to open up Karnak?" Aamira asked.

"Yes," Adewara said, "Our only way into Karnak is through the blood of the sacred. Karnak was kept a secret to protect the chosen bloodlines from having a place to dwell and heal after four hundred years of exile from their homeland of Sahael and Alkebulan."

"I don't even know what to do," Aamira said, looking at

the people as they gathered nearer.

After several minutes, a woman and man approached Adewara, Aamira, and Abioye with a few guards protecting them. They were covered from head to toe in sand blankets and goggles.

They removed their gear, revealing fine robes of bright color with golden jewelry. Without needing to ask, Aamira assumed these were the rulers of IFF, King Ayotunde and Queen Adana.

"Son!" The queen cried as she hugged Abioye. The king limped forward as well and embraced his son. Aamira couldn't help but think the king looked sick and weak. His complexion almost gray; his eyes a pale yellow.

"I thought the worst, that you were dead, Father," Abioye said.

"I'm fine, but my time is fading," King Ayotunde said.

Queen Adana immediately noticed Aamira's Emerald eyes and greeted her with open arms as the royals both embraced her.

"The Signs of the Times are upon us," Queen Adana said. "The land is shifting as Aarde changes before our very eyes. You, Princess of Sahael, your being here is a threat, hope, and blessing to every Yoruban. These people are in fear that they'll be wiped out if General's Scipio's scouts and men return unexpectedly. You bring great danger here."

"It's not my fault all of you chose to come here," Aamira said defensively. She wasn't about to take credit for them rushing off into the desert to a door they couldn't open. "I'm following Solomon's councils, that's all. Your choices are your own."

"The people are here because of you, Aamira," Adewara said.

"Can you help save these people and get them into

Karnak?" Queen Adana asked. She walked to the entrance of Karnak, placing her hand on the solid stone. "You were chosen for this. Solomon told us all of this would happen. He spoke to my husband and I, saying that when rebellion spread across the lands, Aarde itself would shake and betrayal would come from all sides. At that moment, the righteous were to flee to Karnak, where within two days, the Princess of Sahael would arrive to open the door. As it was promised, so has it occurred. The earthquakes began with a cry of rebellion. Our vizier led a rebellion of unbelievers against us, forcing us to flee here, and within two days of our arrival at the Nairo Gate, you stumble out of the desert with our son. Ishtar and Obatala be praised!"

"Ishtar and Obatala be praised!" the people shouted. Their voices echoed through the canyon, reverberating as if repeated a thousand times.

The echoing seemed to go on forever in Aamira's mind. She had gone from a comfortable, weak young woman, to an angry vengeful one, and now being seen as a savior by people she had never met. For a moment she wished she was back at the plantation playing cards with Braémah and eating puffed tarts from the kitchen.

'I don't know what to do," Aamira repeated.

Adewara motioned toward the giant stone door with both hands. "None of us do. But we have faith the gods know and have prepared the way for you."

Aamira nodded and walked up to the entrance. As she approached, her tattoos started to glow, as did the markings on the door. The gathered crowd collectively gasped. A tear trickled down the cheek of Queen Adana. Aamira's eyes lit up and she could feel the power in the rocks around her. If she had wanted, she could have pulled the walls down all around them and buried an army if needed.

The entrance suddenly became transparent, as if made of air. Aamira stretched her hand out to touch the rock, but they passed through the doorway. The people started to rejoice.

"Thank you for opening the gates into Karnak!" Queen Adana shouted. She turned to the people. "Please follow me."

No one moved.

"It's okay you all can enter," Queen Adana said.

The people still wouldn't enter, looking to Aamira for guidance.

Adewara stepped forward. "King Ayotunde and Queen Adana, with all due respect, the two of you have no authority to command the people to enter Karnak." He turned to Aamira. "You are who the people have been waiting for. They will be watching what you do next."

King Ayotunde and Queen Adana looked around confused.

"Please help us understand," King Ayotunde said.

"The Chosen right of Election resides within Aamira's bloodline," Adewara said. "The people will only listen to you, Aamira."

Savior. Leader. Chosen Blood. They were just words. Aamira was none of them. Despite her trepidation, she nodded her head.

"Please enter everyone," Aamira said. She started walking, passing through the transparent gates.

The people followed.

Beyond the gate, canyon walls opened up even further, revealing a city of yellow stone buildings nestled in a massive rock cove with dunes above. Aamira guessed that from up in the desert above, you would not be able to see the depression housing the city unless you fell into it. The city itself was expansive. Light from the hot sun reflected off glass windows in the buildings, evidencing the skill with which it was built. It wouldn't have surprised Aamira to learn a million people could live here safely. With the few thousand there now, finding room for everyone would be no problem.

"This will be our home until the time comes for us to leave this place," Queen Adana said. "So long as Princess Aamira proclaims it so. In the meantime, we will continue to accept the remnants of the lost and scattered people all over the desert."

Adewara, Abioye, and Aamira spoke with King Ayotunde and Queen Adana as the people were entering.

"There are important matters that need to be discussed," King Ayotunde said. "General Scipio is planning to destroy those who share the sacred blood in all the cities in the Desert Sand Lands. Vizier Abdul Hussien has allied with the general and promised to hold Beth-din, so the people have nowhere else to go. His betrayal, while not shocking to those of us who served with him for the past 20 years, is still a blow we hoped would never fall. General Scipio sent assassins in an effort to kill us both after the land started to shift."

"In an effort to help save the people in the other cities," Adewara replied, "we need to save those that share the sacred blood. Due to the fact that General Scipio will not be able to distinguish between those of the sacred bloodline and those of other family lines, he will kill every black person to ensure he exterminates everyone who shares sacred Yoruban blood."

"The people need to find their way to Karnak sooner rather than later," Queen Adana said. "And hopefully not lead Scipio here in the process."

"That may be unavoidable. Mother," Abioye warned.

"Necolyte's prophecy of the people returning to Karnak is

happening," Adewara said as a family passed by laughing and singing as they entered Karnak. "A series of irreversible events starting with the signs of the times. When the earthquakes started last month, word also came of the shifting of ocean currents. General Scipio's mandate to eradicate the sacred blood and the enslaved people on IFF is a reaction to the world changing. Lord Commander Natas knows his mission is to destroy Sahael, while he was successful in destroying the cities and leaving the land uninhabitable, he was unsuccessful in that the princesses survived."

"How are we to deal with these obstacles while having to prevent the extinction of our people?" Queen Adana asked.

Aamira wanted to say something but was cut off by Adewara

"Aamira is the Black Madonna of the Yoruban bloodline; possessing the sacred right to lead the sacred bloodline back to Sahael," Adewara explained. "This isn't about challenging your authority to rule in Karnak, your highness, but it is not your right to do so. It is Aamira's."

Just as Aamira opened her mouth to protest, King Ayotunde suddenly dropped to his knees.

"Father!" Abioye cried.

"I'm sorry...my son," the king gasped. "I wanted to be strong for...you."

Tears fell freely from Queen Adana's eyes. "Your father was poisoned in the city of Beth-din by one of General Scipio's spies, and Vizier Hussein himself. He's dying and doesn't have much time."

"We need to get him to a healer!" Abioye shouted, drawing the attention of the people still streaming into Karnak through the gate. "Call someone! Adewara, you know of herbs as an Educator.

Do something!"

Adewara knelt down and examined the king's eyes. He stood and shook his head. "It was Araban Root. Once it's in someone's system it invades the organs, taking days to kill its victim. Scipio and Hussein chose well in their weapon. I am sorry. Even if we'd arrived yesterday, there would have been nothing I could do."

Abioye cried as he held his father.

"I stayed strong…until I could see you again…Abioye," King Ayotunde said, voice weak and gravely. His skin became even more ashen as he spoke, as if the will to keep himself alive faltered.

"We will see your father's plan through. It's what he wanted for the people," Queen Adana said.

"I failed, Father," Abioye wept. "You sent me to assassinate the Lalaurie woman, but I failed. I failed you."

"You…didn't fail. You brought us…the Princess of…Sahael. It was the will…of Ishtar…and Obatala. You are…not…fail…"

The king coughed and closed his eyes. He never spoke again, dying in Abioye's arms after a few moments of silence.

They burned King Ayotunde's body outside the Nairo Gate doors. Smoke rose into the air, catching currents that floated fumes into the sky.

Adewara stood next to Aamira as the royal family

mourned. Abioye seemed particularly broken by the passing of his father. At least one hundred people stood around weeping and howling in respect to their king.

"This was a mistake," Adewara whispered to Aamira.

"What do you mean?" Aamira replied quietly.

"Look at the smoke. Even an untrained soldier in Scipio's army could see that plume. Burning of the deceased is tradition, and the queen was adamant despite my protests. We need to be extra wary in the coming days. This…performance puts us all in danger."

Aamira knew that she needed to tread lightly and remained quiet for now. Abioye and his mother needed time to mourn. Aamira needed to watch her every move from now on. She had met many 'high-born' individuals as she traveled with the Lalaurie family to events like the Royal Rumble. High-born 'nobles' always got their way, and the people below them suffered for it. Aamira had been one of them, after all.

Was she still? Did she want to be comfortable and pampered?

No.

She wanted to rage and kill and release the pent-up anger of an entire generation.

That girl who used to live in the manor and watch the slaves from afar was gone, now replaced by a determined woman with the power to shake all of Aarde.

And Aarde would shake.

CHAPTER III
ENLIGHTENED KNOWLEDGE

Karnak, The Desert Sand Land of IFF

Months after settling into Karnak, Yoruban stragglers started making their way to the legendary sanctuary. The people who had entered with Aamira and the royal family grew accustomed to their new home. They were able to farm land inside of Karnak as water ran continuously through aquifers below the city's surface.

General Scipio's troops patrolled the desert around Karnak tirelessly, picking off groups of careless refugees. They seemed to have discovered the general area where the city resided, but never drew close enough to actually find the entrance or the hidden valley.

While a self-sustaining paradise, the caveat was that the people inside were permanently trapped. Karnak was built on top of Cheops pyramid, an underground city built by the Egyptians before they were wiped out by the Ukáváál in the ancient times.

Tremors regularly shook Karnak; not enough to destroy buildings, but enough to remind everyone that Aarde was in a state of upheaval. The people prayed regularly in mass communion for protection.

For three months Aamira stayed out of Queen Adana's way. The queen spent most of her time in the temple of Karnak mourning her husband. She was firm and immovable. Aamira knew that eventually the two women would butt heads, which could lead to a division among the people. The longer that eventuality remained a possibility as opposed to a reality, the better.

Adewara kept Aamira busy as she struggled to learn more about her purpose and role among the people she was now served.

"I want to know and understand the history of why the Yorubans were brought to the Desert Land Sands of IFF," Aamira said as she sat with Adewara in the library of Karnak. While most of the books had become desiccated and brittle over the centuries, some were written on plates of ore or thick animal skins, allowing them to have survived the abandonment of Karnak. She had read what she could, but much of the history was woefully out of date.

"Your curiosity has grown," Adewara said as he scratched at his graying beard. "You say that you never really listened to Solomon as he taught you after the Royal Rumble, but I find that hard to believe with the number of questions you ask of this humble Educator."

Aamira smiled. She sat down, hoping to be taught by Adewara. "I'm not a spoiled, fearful girl anymore. At least I hope I'm not."

"You've definitely grown in the three months since we met. And when once more you are reunited with your princess cousins, hopefully in the splendor of the city of Sahael, they won't recognize you as the girl you once were."

Adewara sat down in a polished wooden chair and leaned toward Aamira.

"And now, I will answer your question. After the Invasion of Sahael, all Yorubans, Orishans, Hausans, and Demirrians were taken from their homes as the Narsans invaded three of the Quad-

Cities. These four bloodlines were placed in large obsidian cages and then delivered to the Desert Sand Lands of IFF, The Mountainous Lands of Nuberia, Iceoth, and Ketta Island, forced to never leave. Lord Commander Natas ordered Abingdale, Lucedale, and Vannadale to patrol and monitor their shores and Islands, ensuring that the Yorubans would be watched over until their destruction."

Aamira listened intently. "Tell me more. Sahael's history is vast. Learning all of this is going to be a lot of work."

Adewara chuckled. "The history of Sahael is indeed vast, but important to know. And I'm glad you're so interested. Prior to the Narsan invasion, all Sahaelians traveled through the Nairohenge Gates to A.M.I.T. where the library city of Timbuktu is located. Timbuktu is the center of all knowledge. It's where all Black people are taught about their true history away from witan interference."

"It's where you Educators study, right?" Aamira asked.

"That is correct," Adewara nodded. "It is a beautiful place, and it has been some decades since I've been there. Witans do all within their power to prevent our true history from being shared in Aarde. That paints them as the devils they are, taking what they think is theirs as they appropriate our culture and other cultures. They have none of their own, so they steal from others."

"I've noticed and have experienced all of that growing up in Vannadale," Aamira said. "Witans used the enslaved people to entertain them in all ways."

"Let's change the topic for now and focus on your history," Adewara said. "Before Sahael's Invasion, Obatala and Ishtar established the ancient order in the city of Katunkumene on the planet of Andalusia; from the Ancient Order, Obatala and Ishtar sent down the Watchers to act as sentries over the four realms in Aarde."

"That last time I heard those names was when my cousins and I were in the Aban province; speaking to Solomon in his personal tent," Aamira said.

Adewara handed Aamira a leather book with beautiful green and gold embossing on the cover. It was heavy, containing pages beyond count.

"This is a copy of Necolyte's journal," Adewara explained. "I want you to read it as much as you can once we're done speaking today. Here, let me add some visual aids to our discussion."

Adewara stood and brought over a chalkboard with an image of Aarde on the black surface, showing the four realms created by the Watchers. Aamira looked at the chalkboard seeing how Adewara quickly numbered the four realms.

"The four realms in Aarde were located in the North, East, West, and South," Adewara said.

"Let's start in the North," Aamira said.

"Very good. Nier's Realm is located deep in the North and is responsible for all of the life magic poured into Aarde to bless the people in Alkebulan, and Black people all over Aarde." Adewara explained.

"Tell me about the realm in the East," Aamira said.

"That's Neros's Realm, accountable for all life energy poured into the spirits of Aarde so that all Alkebulan spirits had bodies of flesh to dwell inside of after their birth. The west is Nethal's Realm, responsible for the life essence entering into Aarde for the Alkebulan people. Nethal's Realm protects the soul after it's created when life energy enters Alkebulan bodies. The uniting of the body and spirit is what creates the souls of Black Alkebulans and Sahaelian children."

"I see that there's a wall that separates three realms in

Eastern Aarde from the realm in Western Aarde," Aamira recognized.

Adewara nodded and pointed to the drawing of a divide on the map. "Good eye. The wall that splits Aarde into two is known to all as the Nibiru Wall. Naharis's Realm is located deep in the south and is responsible for the Death Magic. Death Magic allows Naharis's Realm to track the bodies of the dead, allowing them to hear Nova's song. The Vitiligo Knights travel all over Aarde using their Chalcedony rings to open portals of Nebuchadnezzar to bury the dead beneath Deliquesce's seal with no need of bringing them back to Naharis's realm." Adewara paused and glanced toward the door. "I need to meet with the queen. Read what you can while I'm gone. There is more knowledge here than I could ever teach in a day or a year. I'll be back."

After Adewara stepped out, Aamira got up and observed the murals on the south wall, images depicting what Adewara had been explaining. She walked around Karnak's vast twelve-storied library seeking any information she could find on her family's deep history. She knew the books would be centuries out of date, but they may contain glimmers of the past that could help her.

Aamira walked through the library and wiped the cobwebs off several books. She coughed because of the dust in the air. One book caught her eye, and she pulled it from the shelf; *The Watchers Complete History and Genealogy: a Comprehensive Account of the Sacred Yoruban Bloodline.*

She sat back down and opened the book, reading from the first page.

'After the watchers were sent down to Aarde, Obatala & Ishtar established realm laws written by the Nairobians in Katunkumene preventing Naharis's realm from retrieving Black Alkebulan bodies and taking them back to Naharis's Realm, or any realm for that matter. After the four watcher realms were set and

established, Obatala and Ishtar sent down the four chosen bloodlines.'

"This is fascinating!" Aamira gushed, voice echoing through the quiet library. She continued reading.

'The Negralli were sent to Nier's realm, in the North, where they were blessed with magical abilities to help serve and enhance the lives of the Alkebulan people. They were distinguishable amongst the Alkebulans by their sapphire-colored eyes. Once they merged their bloodlines with the Nephilim, their gifts were enhanced, creating the Orishan Bloodline. The Anunnaki were sent to Neros's realm, in the East, where they were blessed with the power of Life Energy by breathing Life into the Sahaelian and Alkebulan children after they left the womb. They were responsible for protecting Black life in all its colors, shapes, and shades. The Anunnaki were distinguishable by their Emerald eyes after merging bloodlines with the Negrunde and inheriting each other's gifts. This merging created the Yoruban bloodline.'

Aamira read for hours waiting for Adewara to return. When he finally did, he brought food with him and placed fresh fruit and vegetables on a nearby table.

"I brought something for you to eat," Adewara said. "The trees and gardens are flourishing despite the heat. I need to go out into the desert and kill some snakes and lizards for meat, but for now, this will do. I see you've been reading quite a bit. Shall we continue our lesson?"

"Yes!" Aamira said enthusiastically. "All of this is so exciting to learn. I've been reading about the creation of the Bloodlines."

"Let's continue with the world and how each realm interacts. The third realm in Eastern Aarde, Nethal's Realm, is where Ishtar and Obatala sent the Elohim, who were blessed with protecting the bonding essence of the souls, joining together the

Alkebulan peoples and preventing them from being corrupted," Adewara explained.

"That sounds serious," Aamira said. "I read that the Watchers of Nethal's realm had a tremendous number of responsibilities. Could this have affected them?"

Adewara nodded. "They worked to prevent the wandering and impure spirits from entering the souls of newborn Alkebulan children. They were distinguishable amongst the Alkebulans because they all had Hematite gray-colored eyes after merging bloodlines and becoming the watchers. They inherited wonderful gifts though. Their merged bloodlines created the Hausan. The mixing of their blood created a unique genetic anomaly, in that soon after birth, they sprouted large wings from their backs and eventually gained the ability to fly."

"That's what Solomon told us," Aamira remembered. "He said my cousin, Heziara, had wings that were hidden. They would manifest at the right moment once again and she would be able to fly. That sounds like an amazing gift!"

Aamira's mind flooded with memories of her cousins, whom she considered sisters. Oadira and Heziara were somewhere out there in Aarde. Had their powers manifested as hers had? Were they safe and happy? Was Heziara flying at that very moment? She longed to see both of them again.

Adewara grabbed the last of the four books on the table Aamira had been reading.

"Ahh, this is a good one," he said. "Have you had a chance to look through it?"

"Not yet."

"Well, then let me teach from its pages. I must admit, as an Educator, there is nothing we like more than an apt pupil." Adewara opened the book and placed it in front of Aamira. "The

Last of the Watchers was the Nelioans who were responsible for escorting the bodies of the dead, to their homelands and burying them below Deliquesce's Seal. They would then help escort their spirits to Naharis's Realm through Nullify's Gate to rest for all eternity. They were distinguishable amongst the Alkebulans with turquoise eyes after merging with the Egyptians and becoming the Demirrians; Watchers of the Southern Realm."

"What happened to all of them?" Aamira asked.

"At one point, they lived and dwelt on the Alkebulan continent for specified amounts of time but were never permitted into the city of Sahael. The realms, however, were to remain in the shadows looking out for Sahael, Alkebulan, Egyptus, and Horn in unison, monitoring Aarde.

"It was their duty and responsibility, given by Obatala, Ishtar, and the ancient Kemite leaders who helped write the Nairobi laws. After the war in Katunkumene to help solidify their eternal agreement, Ishtar and Obatala asked the ancient Kemite leaders Kainoa and Kaimana to send the other Kemites to create seals for all four of the Realms in Aarde on Nullify's Gate. They created Neolithic's chamber, Norms Door, Nullify's Gate, Nectanebo's Key slots, Nabopollassar's seals, and Nebuchadnezzar's portals. Nier, Neros, and Nethal agreed that Naharis' realm needed to be watched because of the potential for Hosts to sneak through Nullify's Gate and not be contained in Neolithic's chamber, getting past Norm's door."

Footsteps interrupted the lesson. Aamira turned to see Abioye entering the library.

"My mother asked that I check on the two of you," Abioye said, grabbing an apple from the table and taking a bite.

"I just spoke with her a half hour ago," Adewara said. "Does she not trust my teaching? Or did she send you here to learn more about your history? You were never as attentive during your studies as I would have liked."

"And now I'm regretting it," Abioye said, taking a seat across from Aamira. "Now that my father is gone, people are looking to me to lead. I feel…unprepared. Maybe it's a good idea I listen a bit. I heard you mention the Hosts. Please continue."

"Of course, that would be what you want to hear about," Adewara said, shaking his head. "Queen Adana forbids me teaching any of the royal court about the Hosts, not wanting to get caught up in the deep dark history. Your mother knows and understands the aspects of the past that could throw you off your own path?"

"What path?" Prince Abioye asked. "The straight and narrow? I'm not a child anymore. And didn't you always tell me that knowledge would open the door to wisdom? Don't I need wisdom now more than ever?"

"This dark history goes deeper than just Hosts," Adewara warned. "The plan to abolish enslavement trafficking, which you are now tasked with doing in your father's stead, needs to be done for reasons bigger than you could ever imagine. The Black females and some of the Black males are systematically being killed through the trafficking trade. Their bodies are being taken by the Ennead to Naharis's realm to have their bodies used for the Hosts…" Adewara paused, taking a breath.

"Who are the Hosts?" Aamira asked, with a look of innocence on her face. "This is knowledge we both need to know. I'm not a member of the court, so teaching me won't break any rules."

"And I'm seen as the heir to my father, the King," Abioye added. "Shouldn't the king know the dark dangers of the world?"

Adewara sat down at the table with Aamira and Abioye, rubbing his forehead. "There were spirits cast out of the presence of Obatala and Ishtar for fighting against their plan for mankind on Aarde. That rebellion from before the word existed led to a civil war. The divines offered a method to their children that would allow them to come to Aarde, save the Kemites, and experience what it means to be Aardian. They wanted their children to learn how to deal with failure, success, pain, and anger; to understand their true purpose. They were all allowed reentry back into Katunkumene if they followed the directions and dictates outlined for them by allowing them the opportunity to have free will to choose for themselves."

"Those terms don't sound so bad," Aamira said.

"They don't at all," Abioye agreed.

Adewara cleared his throat. "The only catch was that those who chose the plan would have no recollection of Katunkumene, which caused many spirits to pause and rethink their allegiance to the plan. Lord Commander Natas, Ishtar and Obatala's eldest son, had a plan of his own, guaranteeing everyone returned to the Eternal Lands as long as they gave up their free will and all of the glory of their deliverance went to him."

"I can see how that could be tempting," Aamira said. "For a long time, I didn't want any choices at all, so long as I felt safe and comfortable in the Madame's house. Choices felt like too much responsibility."

"It was indeed tempting," Adewara confirmed. "So tempting, one-third of the Katunkumene's liked Lord Natas's plan so much, they rebelled against the wisdom of Ishtar and Obatala. Two-thirds of the Andalusians didn't like Natas' plan and sided with their celestial creators. Civil war began and ended after an eternity of conflict."

"Is this the same Lord Commander Natas that invaded Sahael?" Aamira asked, concerned.

"Yes," Adewara said. "The same one you and your cousins encountered at the Coliseum of El Djem during the Royal Rumble where you met Solomon the protector of Aarde."

"It's a miracle he never found us," Aamira said, shaking her head. She and her cousins had gotten so close to being discovered. Natas would have shown them no mercy.

"That must have been terrifying," Abioye replied. "I've never been through anything like that…until now of course. It makes you reevaluate a lot of things. Being hunted by someone like Natas would sap all hope. I'm glad you made it through."

He looked truly concerned as he spoke. Perhaps losing his father had humbled Abioye. Aamira hoped so. The man she had met during the rebellion would not have made a good king at all. This more introspective version would do far better.

Adewara continued. "Abioye is right. You and your cousins can thank your mothers and your fathers for your survival. Their rings and bracelets kept you all hidden right under Lord Commander Natas's watchful eye. They gave their very lives to bring it about. It was powerful magics that only blood ransom can conjure. Another reason why you need to figure out a way to get to Sahael, to make their sacrifice worth it."

"How did Natas come down to Aarde in the first place?" Aamira asked.

"Ishtar and Obatala cast out Lord Natas, their oldest, from Katunkumene. He was thrown into the Nothing, one of the four realms of Outer Darkness, after judgments were handed down by the Judges Anubis and Nineveh. They were eventually cast out as well according to the Nairobi laws," Adewara explained, rubbing his hands nervously. "Lord Commander Natas somehow escaped his exile and made it into Aarde. He's been waiting and wanting to prove to his parents that his plan was the right plan all along. He once was beautiful and peaceful. Now he is vengeful and cankered.

His presence in Aarde means terrible and evil things are on the horizon. I don't know what they are. I fear no one truly does."

Aamira's heartbeat faster. "You mentioned seals. Those seals were also discussed in one of the volumes I've been reading. If he's in Aarde, perhaps he destroyed seals, and moved through them?"

"There is no way Lord Commander Natas could have destroyed the seals; they were created to prevent him and the Hosts from entering Aarde," Adewara said.

"What would happen to Aarde if they ever got past the seals that were created to keep them out?" Abioye asked while eating another apple.

"If for some reason the Hosts were to ever find themselves inside of Aarde," Adewara replied, "they would take possession of all the bodies that have died. They would awaken the dead to get them to fight the living. This is why we need to get to Sahael to make sure the seals are in place to prevent it from ever happening."

Aamira continued thinking about her encounter with Solomon when she was in his tent with her sisters. He had told them that she and her cousins would be the ones to bring catastrophic change to Aarde before they could enter Sahael. Were the earthquakes part of this? Were worse things yet to come?

"Why are the signs so destructive to everyone around Aarde?" she questioned. "I have tried to understand them, but I haven't been able to comprehend why they are happening. I've even tried to stop the tremors with my abilities, but I haven't been successful."

"Knowing how many signs there are and why they're important, would be helpful to know," Abioye said. "The people are constantly praying, but their faith is being tested as the earthquakes intensify. This is a city made of sandstone. One massive quake would destroy everything, killing thousands. Their fear is justified."

"The Signs of the Times are centered around the four ancient bloodlines," Adewara replied, taking a bite of dried fruit as well. "They are tied to the events happening in Aarde. The second sign started with ocean currents across the world reversing. This reversal has affected the way the water once flowed, gradually affecting all of the continents in Aarde. In time, you will find out why the signs are important, but for now, let's focus on learning what the signs mean to you and how they can help get you into Sahael. Agreed?"

Abioye chuckled. "One thing you need to know about Educators, Aamira, is that they never give the full answer."

"Not until the student is ready to understand it," Adewara smiled. "An answer is useless if the listener doesn't even understand the question. Let's continue to find what you need to know to fully understand your purpose. For now, we are safe in Karnak. That may not always be the case. Read, study, and work together. The people look to the queen, but also to the two of you. It is a responsibility you may not have asked for or wanted, but it is thrust on you both, nonetheless. Respect it."

Aamira nodded. She was beginning to understand her role. She may not have asked for it, but it was now on her shoulders. Becoming strong enough to shoulder the burden would be her only goal.

CHAPTER VI
THE THREAT WITHIN

Karnak, The Desert Sand Lands of IFF

Aamira, Prince Abioye, and Adewara studied for weeks deep in Karnak's temple, going over scrolls, chronicles, and old parchments. Aamira continued reading and learning about the Signs of the Times, coming away disappointed in how little the volumes contained regarding their details.

"Karnak is beautiful in the afternoon," Aamira said as the three of them sat on a library balcony in the sunlight. People moved around in the city below them, working, farming, and building larger aqueducts to service the growing number of people arriving daily.

"It is," Abioye agreed as he munched a few nuts from the platter in front of them. "The people are serving each other. It's good to see. Yesterday a group of refugees arrived bloodied and hungry. They had lost almost all their husbands and brothers in a fight with Scipio's army. Only through their bravery and sacrifice were the wives and daughters able to escape."

"Scipio draws closer every day," Adewara lamented, eyes fixed on a group of men training with swords in the courtyard below. He looked up at Aamira. "How is your training progressing?"

"Pretty well," she shrugged. "Each morning I practice, just

as you told me. Then I've been spending an hour with the Queen's guard learning how to use the weapons I manifest. I think it's been going okay."

"She's doing well, according to the reports my mother has been reading," Abioye confirmed.

Adewara nodded and looked back down at the soldiers. "Good. Very good. Keep at it."

"The second sign caused the waters to reverse," Aamira said, wanting to return to their studies. "Shortly after that, the third sign started when I caused all the quakes happening everywhere in Aarde. What was the first sign? I can't find records of it."

"Again, I'm grateful you've become so interested in learning," Adewara said. "Unfortunately, we don't know why Necolyte's prophecy starts with the second, third, and fourth signs. I'm sure one day soon it will become clear, but for now, let's focus on what we do know. Aarde quakes are happening because of you, Aamira, and I have to believe that they are happening for a good reason."

Aamira lowered their head in disappointment. She had hoped that by asking the right question, Educator Adewara would give her the answer, not confirm he didn't know. Plus, reminding Aamira of the earthquakes being her fault didn't help.

"Everything will be alright," Adewara said. His words gave comfort to Aamira. "Things are happening that we don't fully understand. I feel that in time we will understand. We have a lot of time to figure things out. This is why we must get to Sahael. Only then will we know."

"These Signs are all centered around ongoing rebellions, right?" Abioye asked.

"Yes, rebellions that will lead to all-out war in the colonies," Adewara said.

"The provinces might remain unscathed throughout this process," Aamira said, pointing at a map of the islands in Eastern Aarde hanging on the wall just inside the library.

"That will be for Alkebulan's three empires to decide," Adewara said.

"Alkebulan, Sahael, Egyptus, and Horn are surrounded by their enemies. Why would a race of witans choose to destroy and exploit the motherland?" Aamira asked.

"I don't know why; this is why we need to get to Sahael," Adewara said.

Aamira had heard these exact words from Solomon. Every day the desire to return to Sahael grew. She knew she needed to get home.

"I want to get back there and end all of this suffering," Aamira said, smacking her hand against the table.

"You have to let it play out naturally," Adewara explained. "All of this is a process set in motion by the Divines. The shifting of the land beneath our feet, the change in the water currents throughout Aarde; all of it is meant to take place. We cannot rush any of this. The signs of the times are happening, and you are in the middle of them. Getting to Sahael is the priority, but circumstances will dictate when that is possible. Trust in Ishtar and Obatala. They will---"

"Our spies have figured out a way to disrupt Vannadale's trafficking ring permanently on the island," a powerful female voice interrupted. "Report to the council room immediately, Adewara and Prince Abioye."

Queen Adana stepped onto the library balcony accompanied by her personal guards.

"My queen," Adewara stood and bowed.

"Leave us," she ordered.

Adewara gave Aamira a side glance, face like stone. "Yes, my queen."

Adewara immediately left.

"The two of you may join us," Queen Adana said. There was no warmth in her eyes like Aamira had seen on that day in the desert standing before the gate to Karnak. The queen had become cold as ice in the months since their arrival.

Abioye and Aamira followed Queen Adana from the library and across the square to the grand hall with its domed ceiling and polished tiled floors. When they arrived, the Queen's council and her leaders were in attendance. An animal skin map of the island of IFF and surrounding continents spread across the large circular table. Small flags marked the locations of the enslavement trafficking camps set up to catch Blacks and take them back to Vannadale.

Queen Adana stood at the head of the council and pointed at the map. "I have a plan designed that will wipe out the witan traffickers on this island for good. It's been reported that the province is wanting to bring their whole operation to our sandy shores while also looking to colonize and enslave all the people here. The intel our spies have gathered include General Scipio enslaving every Black person and impregnate the Black females to place these mixed children into the trade, sending them to Abingdale afterwards.

"The intel your spies have is wrong," Aamira said "Madame Delphine would never set up her operations where you show them on the map. She and I were very close, and I know---"

"You have no voice here!" Queen Adana shouted, voice echoing around the large domed chamber. "Keep your mouth shut!"

The tone in her voice took Aamira aback. Since the king's death, and Adewara's implication that Aamira would be the ruler of the people, not the queen or Abioye, Adana had obviously become openly hostile toward the young woman.

Still, Aamira would no longer be cowed like a weak Heffer. Her pulse quickened and anger of her own flooded her veins.

"What I say is true," she said through grit teeth. "These witans are clever and have a deceptive way of throwing inaccurate information at you that may seem real."

"Again, I remind you, you have no voice here," Queen Adana said.

"I don't need permission from you to speak. If you choose not to listen, you will be walking into a trap."

"The next time you speak out of turn, I'll have you thrown into a cell," Queen Adana threatened.

Members of the council glanced back and forth between each other. Abioye stood silently, staring at the wall across the room from them.

Aamira simply nodded. If this woman had become so lost in her grief and fear that she wouldn't listen to reason, Aamira would let her hang herself.

Queen Adana continued speaking about how the plan to attack would be executed. "We will face them head on and with force, in a surprise attack and wipe them out; it's what King Ayotunde would've wanted for IFF."

Aamira bit her tongue but couldn't keep silent.

"If you attack, then you doom yourself and your army," Aamira said. "I want them dead as much as anyone, but---"

"Guards seize her and place her in the dungeons at once!" Queen Adana ordered. The veins on her forehead and neck tightened like metal cords.

The Emerald guard rushed forward and grabbed Aamira by the arms.

"Abioye!" Aamira cried. "You know this isn't right! Do something."

"Abioye answers to me, and me alone," Queen Adana said. "Son, you are forbidden from being around this rodent of a woman. Aamira is forever sentenced to the sand dungeons, on my order, Queen of IFF; Queen of Karnak."

Aamira had languished in the sandy prison for two months.

Sand caked her hair and skin. Stone walls surrounded her on three sides, with obsidian bars on the fourth that looked out on a sand dune that blocked any view of the city. Day and night, wind would blow granules around the prison, forcing Aamira to close her eyes for long periods of time. She was kept under heavy guard at all times.

"How are you faring?" Adewara asked as he walked up to the bars. It had been several weeks since he had last visited.

"Her royal highness finally let you come back to see me?" Aamira said as she scratched at a patch of rough skin on her arm.

"I am doing what I can."

"Good for you."

Adewara looked Aamira up and down, a frown on his face. "Again, how are you?"

"Well, the floor is sand, I have to kill hundreds of scorpions per day, so I haven't had a good night's sleep since I've been locked up," Aamira answered.

"That mouth of yours is trouble. You need to get a handle on that," Adewara said.

"Go to hell!" Aamira screamed, grabbing the bars in front of Adewara. "I thought you were on my side. How dare you tell me to keep my mouth in check? No! Since the moment I've been here, Queen Adana has wanted to remain in control. I'm a threat to her and she wants to maintain that control no matter what, even if it costs people their lives. I was only telling her the truth."

"You do speak truth," Adewara said, unmoving. "You're the threat within, according to Necolyte's prophecy."

"I'm the threat?" Aamira spat. "So, you're going to keep me in this dungeon forever despite the fact that I did nothing wrong and broke no law?"

"Yes, and the queen will continue to treat you as a threat. The fact that you are behind these bars is a good thing," Adewara said.

"I'm going to pretend like you didn't just say that," Aamira growled. "Are all Educators so two-faced and cowardly?"

Adewara side-glanced at the guards standing at attention on each end of the bars. "As long as you are in here," he spoke quietly, "the queen won't have you assassinated or poisoned. Queen Adana is looking to get married, ensuring the Chosen Right of Election stays with her, preventing Necolyte's prophecy from taking place. She sent an army out against Scipio, and as you warned, they were wiped out. She's trying to consolidate her power as the people have become angry with her over the needless deaths."

"That bitch is clever and ruthless," Aamira spat.

"Indeed, you have your work cut out for you," Adewara

said. "But I have a plan that will ensure the Chosen Right of Election stays with you."

"I don't care about that," Aamira said, shaking her head. "All I want is to get out of here and not let these people get annihilated by Scipio. They lock me up for months and do nothing?"

"The people think you betrayed the queen," Adewara said. "That's what they've been told. Adana's sins should not be placed at their feet."

"And what about your sins?" Aamira shouted. "What about you, Adewara? You pretended to be my mentor. You taught me and I listened like I never listened to Solomon. And now you leave me in here without fighting for me?"

"I…have my reasons," Adewara said after a pause. "Just trust me. And Abioye."

"Abioye?" Aamira laughed. "That coward is exactly what I thought he was the moment we met. A self-centered, power-hungry rodent."

Adewara gripped one of the bars tightly with his right hand. "You know not of what you speak." His voice dropped to just above a whisper. "Abioye has been fighting for you from the moment his mother locked you in here. He's been working with wealthy patrons of the court and the common people, practically preaching your cause. And you'll need him if you want to make it to Sahael." Adewara glanced at the guards again and continued quietly. "You are going to need to marry Abioye."

"What?!?" Aamira shouted.

Grabbing her hand, Adewara continued. "Listen to me. The queen has gone mad. She has spies everywhere. She's already executed three court pages because they defended you. Since the king's untimely death, grief has torn through her mind. She will kill you if needed. She is marrying Themba, ruler of the Inner Shore Desert of IFF, to consolidate her power. This must be thwarted."

"What are you saying?" Aamira asked.

"Trust me. When the time comes, I will have guards loyal to me on duty when the queen comes to gloat. Use your powers to escape and trap her in this cell. Then, we will marry you to Abioye and the circle will be complete. From there, you can go your separate ways if you wish, but the bloodlines must be united, and you must be in control of IFF."

A gust of wind blew sand into the cell. Aamira shook her head. "You don't think I've tried to use my abilities to escape this cell? The obsidian bars are impenetrable to my magics. I've tried shaking the earth, but all it does is threaten to bring the ceiling down on top of me."

"Shake the bars," Adewara whispered.

"What?"

"Shake the bars. That is all I can tell you. I must go. Be prepared. The moment will arrive soon."

As Adewara began walking up the dune, Aamira called out. "Does Abioye know? About all of this…stuff?"

"He's been prepped and will do what he's been told to do," Adewara said.

After he left, Aamira thought long and hard about what Adewara had said. Was Abioye truly on her side against his own mother? Had the two of them been plotting this entire time to get Aamira out and place her on the throne of IFF? She had spent the better part of the last two months cursing Abioye and Adewara right alongside the queen. Perhaps too much of her old self, the thoughtless and lazy Aamira, still resided in her heart. She had seen Adewara as her mentor, and Abioye as at the very least a fellow student. Maybe they were more than that. Maybe they were both staunch allies that were putting their lives on the line to serve not only her, but the greater good.

Marry Abioye, though?

That was a stretch. He was handsome, but love and companionship had never crossed her mind. Still, political marriages happened all the time, even on the LaLaurie estates. If it got her out of this cell and brought peace to IFF, she could do it.

That night Aamira lay down on the sand with her dirty blanket and thought about what Adewara had said. *'Shake the bars.'*

She longed for the moment when she could put that piece of advice into practice.

Aamira awoke the next morning to sand being kicked in her face. She shot up surprised. Standing above her was Queen Adana, an insane smirk on her face.

"Wake up, bitch," the queen spat. "After today you will be an afterthought in the eyes and minds of the Yoruban people. I'll make sure Necolyte's prophecy will be null and void after today. Guards leave us."

The guards immediately left, leaving Queen Adana and Aamira by themselves. Aamira stood, face to face with the queen.

"After today you will no longer be the Black Madonna," the queen continued. "You will be nothing but a memory to the people who followed you through the gates into Karnak."

"Why would you do this? Are you even yourself?" Aamira asked. "You're not the same woman who prayed in faith and praised me on the day we met so many months ago."

"There's more going on than you could ever imagine," Queen Adana said. Her face was calm, as if fully convinced of the righteousness of her actions. "There is a white mist of darkness moving through Aarde, taking over the minds of witans and making them want to eradicate an entire bloodline. What I'm doing is protecting your bloodline. You are too young and inexperienced to lead these people."

"You're misguided and lost," Aamira countered. "Convincing yourself of nothing but lies. Pride has clouded your judgment."

Queen Adana grabbed Aamira's steel bars and leaned closer to speak.

Aamira realized this was the moment.

She grabbed both of the queen's hands and focused her ability to shake the ground on the bars themselves.

"What are you doing?" the queen asked, suddenly frantic.

Remaining silent, Aamira shot vibrations through the obsidian. The queen shouted for the guards, but it was too late. Under the control of her abilities, the bars felt supple in her hands, manipulated as easily as a wet reed.

In a single movement, Aamira pushed the bars aside, spreading them wide enough to step through. Still holding the queen's shaking hands, Aamira twisted, switching places with Queen Adana and throwing her majesty into the cell. Before the queen realized what was happening, Aamira touched the bars once more and vibrated them back into place.

"What?" the queen gasped, eyes darting to the left and right. "How…?"

The guards ran down the dune towards Aamira.

"Do you serve Adewara?" she shouted.

One of the guards bowed his head. "We serve Sahael, and the chosen princesses."

"Good," Aamira smiled. "I need you to guard the queen. Make sure she is safe and comfortable."

"You won't get away with this!" Queen Adana shrieked.

Aamira started walking up the dune, away from the cell. "You betrayed your people. In your madness, you threatened them all with destruction. I hope you come to your senses."

Once through the sandstone gates of the dungeon area, Aamira wasn't quite sure where to go. She was dirty and caked in sand. People would notice her easily, and she wasn't sure how they would react after having the queen apparently execute people who even tried to defend her.

The answer to her question came swiftly as Adewara stepped from below a shadowed archway to her right.

"You figured out how to escape," Adewara said.

"What do we do next?" Aamira said.

"Follow the plan."

"What plan?" Aamira asked. "You want me to marry Abioye, but it's the queen that's getting married. Beyond that, I have no idea what to do. The queen is in my cell right now. Eventually guards loyal to her will come by and let her go."

"Not if you shape shift to look like her and tell them not to," Adewara smiled.

"I've never done that before," Aamira admitted. "Solomon told me it would hurt, and so I planned on never doing it."

"Pain is a part of life."

"How do I even do it?"

Adewara shrugged. "I don't know. Only you and your sisters can access the ability. But I tell you know, if you pull from your inner strength, you can accomplish anything. I'll do what I can for you on my end, but if we want this to succeed, Queen Adana must stay in that cell until tomorrow. Come to the ceremony wearing her wedding robes and veil. No one will see your face."

"What about this Themba guy she's marrying?"

"Themba will be taken care of," Adewara assured. "He won't be able to interfere until it's too late. What I need you to do is immediately before the ceremony, make an announcement as the Queen that you and Themba have decided that Aamira and Abioye are to be married instead to fulfill the prophecies and lead the people to Sahael. Such an announcement will bring joy and excitement. No one will question it. And once everything comes out, the queen and Themba will have no argument to challenge the marriage since the uniting of the bloodlines was foretold. It doesn't mean there won't be dangers, and even the possibility of bloodshed afterward, but it will be set in stone that you and Abioye are the rulers of IFF, and the protectors of the Alkebulan people on the continent. I will see you tomorrow at the wedding."

Adewara walked away quickly as to not draw any attention to himself.

Aamira stood there in the shadows of the alcove, brain twisting with everything Adewara had just told her. Marriages and announcements and bloodshed. It all seemed too much and to have come and gone too quickly.

What was her role in all this? What was her responsibility to these people? She wanted revenge on the witans, yes, but now she would be ruler and seen as protector.

One thing at a time, she told herself. *Shapeshifting. None of this will work unless you can figure out how to shapeshift.*

She breathed, imaging how she might shapeshift into someone else. Aamira decided to focus on what Solomon had always said about calming the mind and letting instinct take over. As she did, Nebiriau's bracelet lit up along with the tattoos on Aamira's arms.

Pain like she had never felt suddenly ripped through her body. She fell to her knees and gasped. Every cell in her body burned.

Aamira opened her eyes, looking up at the stone archway above her. Had she passed out?

"My queen!" she heard someone shout.

Several guards rushed over and helped Aamira to her feet.

"My queen. Are you alright?" a tall guard in ceremonial armor asked. "Did you fall? Why are you dressed in these rags?"

Aamira looked down at her hands, seeing lines and veins in them that hadn't existed before.

"Queen Adana," the second guard said. "Are you alright?"

Queen Adana?

In that moment, Aamira realized her shape shifting efforts had worked. She looked like the queen.

She had to think fast.

"I'm…fine," Aamira said, voice slightly higher. It was Queen Adana's voice.

"Are you sure, my queen?"

"Yes," Aamira said, brushing their hands from her arms. "I don't need your support."

"Where are your royal robes?" the guard asked, face confused.

"I am mourning my husband!" Aamira said loudly. "I am as low as the dirt itself! Now leave me! And I order no one to relieve the guards currently watching Aamira's cell. I will send Adewara to speak with them. He must learn his place in Karnak. Go!"

The Emerald guards rushed off with a bow.

Aamira smiled. This plan of Adewara's just might work. All she needed to do was go to the queen's quarters, change her clothes, and throw a wrench in the woman's plan to upset the prophecy.

Tomorrow she would disrupt a wedding, and no one would know until it was too late.

This was going to be fun.

CHAPTER IV
THE CHOSEN RIGHT OF ELECTION

Karnak, The Desert Sand Land of IFF

The wedding ceremony of Queen Adana to Themba of the Inner Shore Desert of IFF was unexpectedly postponed. The queen herself, much to the surprise and joy of the people, had announced that it would be Abioye and Aamira who would be marrying. She even went so far as to apologize that she had imprisoned Aamira, saying how badly she felt and that it was her grief that had made her do it.

Aamira tried her best to speak as the queen would, but at one point when she said, "Princess Aamira is a treasure and I love her," she almost started laughing in spite of herself.

No one suspected any foul play, nor seemed to notice Queen Adana had seemingly disappeared after making the announcement.

The Griots were in attendance singing, dancing, and speaking poetry. The most important people in Queen Adana's circle were all in attendance, eating, drinking, and being merry in every way. Hundreds of wild boars, goats, and pigs were on spits rolled over hot coals and cooked to perfection; everyone drank

Amarula, the drink of choice.

Adewara was to officiate the wedding ceremony. As the Educator of the royal court, such was the tradition. The Emerald guard helped with security, ensuring there were no distractions or interruptions. The chairs were set up for the people to attend and be part of the festivities when the ceremony started.

The bells started ringing, signifying that the wedding ceremony was beginning. Adewara stood at the table at the end of the aisle waiting for the bride and groom who were to appear one at a time at the opposite of the aisle thirty yards away. The altar was shaped like a bowl, with four different sections.

The music started.

Aamira walked down the aisle toward Adewara, wearing the same dress and face-covering veil Queen Adana would have worn. For a moment, she wondered what Adewara had done with the original groom, Themba. She knew she would find out eventually. For now, her focus was required elsewhere.

Abioye appeared at the far end of the aisle as well and approached Aamira. He was smiling, dressed in a handsome robe with red and gold inlays over a tan tunic. He looked kingly and attractive. Aamira blushed slightly at his visage.

As the groom, Abioye lifted Aamira's veil. The crowd gasped, whispering of the princess' beauty.

As was tradition, Aamira knelt before her future husband as a sign of submission to her protector.

Abioye remained stoic and steadfast.

They both started walking down the aisle at the same time, in-step with each other. Flower girls tossed emerald-green roses at their feet. The bride and groom made it to the end of the altar.

Adewara smiled, lifting the cloth covering over the four

elements that would symbolically unite the betrothed.

"I welcome you all here this day," Adewara said, voice echoing through the Karnak royal hall. "The two people you see before you, Prince Abioye Adesola and Princess Aamira of Sahael, are an example of love, perseverance, dedication, and strength. They stand before us ready to lead the Yoruban bloodline into the unknown. Princess Aamira, Prince Abioye, the queen has publicly blessed this marriage. We will now begin the ceremony of the Tasting."

Eight spoon bearers rushed forward, dressed in ceremonial robes.

"The Ritual known as the Tasting of the Four Elements is a tradition to fulfill the Yoruban soul," Adewara pronounced, arms outstretched. "The couple will be approached by two of the spoon bearers at the same time. The spoon bearers will stand directly in front of the bride and the groom and kneel as a sign of respect. The bride and the groom will take the spoon and at the same time dip them into the first element. Then together, turn to face each other and place the first element in each other's mouths."

The drums started. signifying the ritual had begun.

Aamira and Abioye did as commanded, taking a spoonful of the first element of sapphire Cayenne and placing a spoonful in each other's mouth.

"The first element is sapphire cayenne symbolizing spiciness in the beginning of your marriage. The passions will be strong and will be needed to strengthen your marriage as you're learning how to deal with outside influences that will surely come to the both of you as newlyweds," Adewara said.

Aamira tasted the sapphire cayenne put in her mouth. It's heat seemed to fill her entire body. She longed for water, but also felt suddenly intoxicated to a small degree.

"You both are to deal with this heat and suffer through it without using water to alleviate the intensity of the cayenne," Adewara continued. "The bride and the groom suffer through the first element together."

They both removed the spoons and placed them back on the pillows of the spoon bearers, who stood from kneeling and returned to the back of the line behind the other spoon bearers.

The second set of spoon bearers approached Aamira and Abioye and kneeled respectively.

The drums continued beating in unison.

"Please partake of the second element," Adewara ordered.

Aamira and Themba did as ordered, taking a spoonful of the second element: emerald lime juice. A sour tang filled Aamira's mouth, along with the warm intoxication she had felt before.

"The second element is emerald lime juice, symbolizing sourness. This taste is to prevent your marriage from ever becoming sour throughout your time together as the both of you face trials and tribulations in the beginning of your marriage. To prevent the sourness, communication must always be at the forefront to ensure that your marriage will always remain steadfast and strong."

The bride and groom's mouths puckered as they turned to face each other and Adewara once again.

"You both are to deal with this sourness and suffer through it using nothing to alleviate the acidity of the emerald lime juice," Adewara ordered.

The bride and the groom suffered through the second element together.

They both removed the spoons and placed them back on the

pillows of the spoon bearers. Two more soon took the place of the servants, kneeling like the others had.

"Please partake of the third element," Adewara ordered.

Aamira and Abioye did as commanded, taking a spoonful of gray Hematite vinegar.

"The third element is Hematite gray vinegar, symbolizing bitterness that has the potential to creep into your marriage if the two of you don't submit to each other. Preventing this taste of bitterness to come between the two of you will strengthen your marriage as difficult choices will have to be made that have the potential of causing division."

Aamira tasted the Hematite gray vinegar. The flavor was hard to describe, but it was every bit as distasteful as the other elements.

"You both are to deal with this and suffer through it without using water to alleviate the intensity of the vinegar," Adewara said.

The last set of ring bearers approached and kneeled respectively.

The drums continued beating louder.

"Please partake of the last element," Adewara ordered.

The last element was different from the others, sweet turquoise liquid candy melts. Aamira smiled as the sweet flavor washed away the unpleasant taste of the previous elements.

"The last element is turquoise liquid candy melts symbolizing sweetness that is to be the priority of your marriage in the beginning, until the end of the time," Adewara grinned. "Happiness must be the backbone of your marriage no matter the circumstances and difficulties that the both of you will face individually and together as newlyweds.

"You both are to deal with this and suffer through it without using anything to alleviate the intensity of the sweetness."

The bride and the groom smiled through the last element together.

The four spoon bearers afterward remained still in their places as the flower girls moved in front of them, sprinkling emerald roses

Adewara walked from behind the altar to address the new Queen and King, along with everyone in attendance.

"By tasting each of these flavors, our new King and Queen Adesola have demonstrated their love for each other and their devotion as newlyweds. This tradition symbolically shows their commitment and devotion to each other. The two of them have demonstrated their ability to remain united for better or worse, for richer or poorer, in sickness and in health, and for time and all eternity. Please, you may kiss each other."

Abioye grabbed both of Aamira's hands and they kissed each other.

The kiss was far more pleasant than Aamira had anticipated. She had never kissed anyone before. She felt a connection to Abioye that hadn't existed prior to this moment.

How strange, she thought. *A few days ago, I felt hatred for him. Now I know Abioye has been fighting for me since the moment I was imprisoned. He is a good man.*

"The spicy, sour, bitter, and sweet stages have all been accepted," Adewara announced. "By the power vested in me, I pronounce you husband and wife, King and Queen on the throne of Karnak and the Sand Lands of IFF, destined to lead our people back to Sahael!"

Everyone rejoiced as the music and festivities started. People cheered and enjoyed the feast. After only a few minutes,

Adewara approached the bride and groom, pulling them away from well-wishers.

"It's Imperative that the two of you get out of here as quickly as possible to consummate your marriage," he counseled giving Abioye the blanket that had covered the altar.

"Consummate?" Aamira whispered. "I thought this was for political purposes, not romance."

The thought of consummating the marriage with Abioye was not something she had considered.

"You must," Adewara stated firmly, looking over his shoulder.

"It's okay if she doesn't want to," Abioye added, face smiling, but obviously hurt by the implied rejection.

Adewara again glanced over his shoulder. "The marriage is not official until it is physically consummated. I can't keep the queen's guards away from your old cell for much longer. Everything will be revealed. They will search and find Themba locked in his quarters. If this ceremony isn't consummated, all will be lost."

Aamira looked at Abioye. She searched her heart. He was good. So much of her thoughts regarding him had been filtered through their first meeting. After their months of studying together, she knew he had matured and grown, just as she had.

The decision was made.

"Let's go," she said, grabbing Abioye's hand.

The guards led them to the bridal chamber where they were immediately met by a group of men and women who were there to help wash and prepare Queen Aamira and King Abioye for their wedding night. They were washed from head to toe in the finest bath oils and fragrances from Aarde.

Afterwards, they were left alone in their chambers. Amira wore an emerald gown. Abioye wore emerald shorts.

"We are finally all alone as King and Queen," Abioye said. "I'm sorry this all happened so fast. I wanted to visit you so many times in the dungeons. I wanted to be there with you, but people were being executed and Adewara advised I---"

Aamira kissed Abioye, stopping his words.

"I know what type of man you are, Abioye," she spoke quietly. "I have held onto hate for a lot of people since the rebellions started and I was forced to accept the real world and not the fake one I had enjoyed my entire life. I'm giving away some of that hate now. Do you accept me as your wife?"

"Yes!" Abioye grinned enthusiastically.

"Then I accept you as my husband."

She pulled one of Njiru's rings from her right hand and placed it on Abioye's finger. The piece of jewelry seemed to swell and change, fitting Abioye's ring finger perfectly.

Another sign Aamira was making the right choice.

They kissed again.

King Abioye lifted up Queen Aamira's gown, as she removed his shorts.

Aamira jumped on Abioye as he held her tight, carrying her to their large, oversized feather bed.

They kissed passionately for a while until Abioye inserted himself into Aamira. As he did, emerald tattoos appeared all over his body for the first time. Aamira's tattoos ignited as well. Njiru's rings glowed, allowing the two of them to be one in mind, body, and soul. As they made love to each other, their minds were connected. They communicated mentally, smiling and laughing with each other, experiencing the four elements of their consummation.

They made passionate love all through the night as the foundations of Karnak shook.

As Adewara had feared, the following morning Queen Adana was released from the dungeons by her very surprised royal guard. She rounded up a contingent of Emerald Guards loyal to her, found Themba locked in his quarters, and immediately went on a rampage.

King and Queen Adesola exited their room for breakfast as Adewara rushed toward them from down the hall.

"Your mother is arriving with Emerald Guards that are loyal to her and Themba," he spoke quickly. "She doesn't look happy at all. We need to be ready to fight to the death."

"Surely it won't come to that," Abioye replied. "My mother has to come to her senses."

Aamira grabbed Abioye's hand. "We need to prepare to fight if your mothers' guards choose not to fall in line with you and I as king and queen."

"We need to find a better way than always resorting to bloodshed," Abioye said.

"I have an idea," Adewara said.

"What do you suggest?" Aamira asked.

"Use your powers and show them you are the Black Madonna. This is for the both of you. You will know what to do when the time is right," Adewara suggested. "Since unifying, you should now possess Yoruban abilities, Abioye. Follow your wife's lead."

Just then, Queen Adana arrived, filling the royal hallway with hundreds of Emerald guards ready to fight.

"Deceivers!" she screamed.

"Mother, this isn't right!' Abioye said.

"This is all due to the Aamira's presence!" Adana spat. "She has tainted you, Son. And you, Adewara. She locked me in a cell, and Themba in his room! She has to go, and you must choose, Abioye, where your loyalties lie. It's her or me. What is it you choose?"

"Aamira," Abioye said without hesitation.

"Attack!" Former Queen Adana cried, pointing at her son.

"Blink your eyes twice!" Adewara said. "Activate your Yoruban gifts!"

Aamira's eyes glowed Zambian along with the tattoos on her body. She glanced at her husband, who now had tattoos and glowing eyes as well. Abioye looked amazed but determined. An indestructible Zambian energetic aura formed around their bodies making former Queen Adana's guards pause for a moment.

"What is going on?" Queen Aamira asked telepathically.

"I don't know," King Abioye said. *"I can hear your thoughts."*

Queen Oadira and King Abioye conjured double-sided Egyptian glaives and charged the former Queen Adana's guards.

"Don't kill them," Abioye said as his blade smashed against the jade breastplate of a soldier, blowing the man aside. *"They're good men, following their queen's orders."*

Nodding, Aamira felt energy flowing through her blade,

exploding against the guards and tossing them like leaves on the wind. After a few moments, Only Queen Adana remained standing.

She pulled a knife from one of the prone guards.

"You'll have to kill me!" she yelled.

The weapons in Abioye's hands dissolved. He walked up to his mother and let her knife touch his chest.

"Mother, I would never hurt you. Seeing you this way over the past few months has been the worst time in my life. But you are wrong. Aamira is the queen. I am king. Such was prophesied by Solomon and the prophets of old. Ishtar and Obatala will it so. If you want to keep fighting and tear this people apart merely for your own pride, don't blame it on your grief for Father's death. This will be your choice, and your folly to explain when you stand before the gods of our ancestors."

Former Queen Adana fell to her knees. She began weeping.

"You truly are the Black Madonna," she whimpered. "I submit to your rule and council, even if it means you require my life for offenses against you."

"That won't be necessary," Aamira said. Why have enemies when you can have loyalties? You're forgiven, Queen mother."

Abioye reached down and pulled his mother from the ground, hugging her close. "And Themba, as Yoruban, is welcomed to stay, Mother. If you wish to marry him still, your King and Queen will allow it."

"As soon as you all are ready over the next several days," Adewara said, sweat dripping from his forehead, "join me in the library. There is much to discuss. For now, though, please go back to your royal quarters. We will have peace among ourselves for as long as peace is an option."

King and Queen Adesola did as ordered. Former Queen Adana walked away. The injured guards slowly returned to their feet and immediately set up watch outside the royal honeymoon chambers. The Emerald guards were now sworn to Aamira.

CHAPTER V
SACRED HISTORY

Karnak, The Desert Sand Land of IFF

Several days later. Aamira and Abioye left the royal quarters and were greeted by cheers from the people gathered outside the central Karnak palace. Joy seemed to permeate the hidden city.

Aamira and Abioye met with Educator Adewara in the library tower. They arrived holding hands.

"I see you both are happy together," Adewara said as he grabbed a large set of thin metal plates held together with brass fittings.

"We are," Aamira smiled.

"So, this isn't just for politics and expedience anymore?" Adewara grinned. "You're not going to run off and fight the witan armies all by yourself?"

"I'm okay right where I am." Aamira snuggled close to Abioye.

"Then welcome, my King and Queen," Adewara said, placing the metal records on the large stone table before them. "I want to congratulate you both on your eternal marriage once more. The undying bond you now share is strong, and there is nothing that can break it between the two of you. You will be tested in ways you'd never thought possible, but through your love and devotion, you both will overcome."

"Adewara, you insisted on wanting to show us something?" Aamira asked.

"Yes," Adewara replied as he opened the metal plates of the record book. "Through study and chance, I discovered that you, Aamira, are from the ancient bloodline of the chosen, who became the Watchers after they were sent down to Aarde by Obatala and Ishtar. They were sent by the leaders Khay and Hemiunu to save the Ancient Kemites after they first arrived by way of Nyathera's asteroid. Ishtar and Obatala sent down four of their grandchildren and their bloodlines to watch over Sahael, Egyptus, and Horn, to protect Alkebulan, and Aarde."

"I'm curious to know what their names were," Aamira said. She believed she knew the answer already but needed confirmation.

"Their names were High Queen Nergal of the Negralli, Great Queen Ninti of the Eloquim, Queen Regent Arishkegal of the Anunnaki, and Queen Morrighan of the Egyptians. Ishtar and Obatala sent them to protect the ancient Kemetic bloodlines of Sahael but also to save the Amun and Aethiopian bloodlines from erasure," Adewara said.

"We need to know which bloodlines were here prior to Nyathera's asteroid and Ishtar and Obatala's actions," Abioye said. "It's what Solomon explained to my father after I left to Vannadale on my mission to destroy Madame Delphine's enslaved trafficking trade."

"Follow me to the other end of the library and I'll show what I've uncovered."

The king and queen followed Adewara from the main

sitting room, down a hall of cracked stone walls. One section opened on a small chamber filled with more brass and silver books like the one Adewara had brought with him. He grabbed a roll of animal skin and unfurled it on a nearby table. It was a map with writing that seemed to flicker and change from moment to moment.

"This is one of Nephrophida's interactive maps," Adewara said. "Nephrophida was a Kemite explorer who surveyed dark space looking for habitable planets ready to be groomed for erasure. This was a destructive thing, but he eventually saw the error of his ways, choosing to renounce and relinquish his role to become a Kemite of peace. Anyways, after your marriage and the numerous quakes, this chamber was revealed."

Adewara pointed at the map of Aarde, showing the four watchers' realms.

"Ishtar and Obatala sent down eight to twelve members of the Katunkumene counsel. The divine's reasons for this were two-fold. First, to create the realms and monuments needed to help protect and bless the people of Sahael and Alkebulan. The second reason was to protect Aarde from threats beyond the stars. The ancients learned that we weren't alone and that world erasers were out in deep space looking to expunge and whitewash Alkebulan history and cultures like the one on Aarde."

"Who were the ones Ishtar and Obatala sent?" Aamira asked, looking over Nephrophida's interactive map.

"According to the changing inscriptions here on the map, they sent Nier and his wife Nereid to create a realm and a monument in the north of Aarde," Adewara said, pointing to the realm and monument. He then tapped his finger against the center of the map. "Then they sent Neros and his wife Nisine to create a realm and monument in the east, on the eastern edges of Aarde. Then the divines sent Nethal and his wife Naré to create a realm and monument in the west, on the western edges of Aarde. Here on the south is where Ishtar and Obatala sent the other members of the Andalusian Council, Naharis and his wife Nablidah, to create a realm and monument on the western edges of Aarde."

"So, we have places of refuge where we can go if needed while trying to regain access to Sahael?" Aamira asked.

Adewara continued. "It's all within their power to help Sahael, Egyptus, and Horn in whatever capacity the two of you are able. The entire continent of Alkebulan is poisoned right now. Natas' attack forced the failsafes to activate. They bleached the skies and left all the lands desolate, even the city of Sahael. Help will be required on every step of your journey. All will need protection against the evils that Aarde will face. The creators of the eight realms, monuments, and builders returned to Katunkumene to help fight in the Katunkumene Wars afterwards."

"What happened after they returned to help fight in the war?" Abioye asked.

Adewara pointed to a section of the map that showed IFF Island. "Before the war on Katunkumene, Ishtar and Obatala sent the chosen bloodlines to mingle with the ancient Kemites to save them from extinction. It initially helped their bloodline, creating a merging with the ancient and chosen lineages. Their individual isolation didn't last long, as one percent of the men and women in the population forced the blinding of the two sexes."

Aamira gasped when hearing what Adewara had said she covered her mouth with both of her in shock.

"Wait, what?" Aamira questioned. "They blinded them? How? Why?"

"Who was responsible for all that suffering?" Abioye asked.

"Damien, the son of Natas, infiltrated the group that was

sent down. He disguised himself as one of the chosen while in Sahael and created disease and parasites designed to fester in females of the chosen bloodlines and males of the ancient bloodlines. Once they married and mingled, blindness would spread among the children. To preserve them, Kainoa and Kaimana, the Supreme leaders of the Kemites, used their technology to travel to Andalusia to hammer out the agreement."

Aamira got up and walked away from the table and the map, overcome by emotion. She was appalled at the idea of that many lives being tormented and lost for no reason at all.

"I need to step away," she said. "Give me some time to think."

She walked through the streets of Karnak in the hot sun, being given fruits and bread from vendors praising her as their queen. These were all wonderful people. How could anyone seek to harm them? Natas' motives seemed completely foreign, until she remembered her own anger and lust for vengeance on the witans who had enslaved and raped her people. She wanted them dead and humiliated. Was this Natas' hatred as well? Was she any better than the demon that had destroyed her homeland?

After a few hours, Aamira returned, ready to hear more of what Adewara had discovered.

"What happened in Katunkumene?" Aamira asked.

"Are you alright?" Abioye asked, rubbing Aamira's shoulder.

"Yes. Let's continue. I have a lot to learn about history and Natas…and myself, I imagine."

"Very good," Adewara said, scratching his graying beard. "Ishtar and Obatala offered a solution to the four most prominent ancient Kemetic bloodlines, that were all males, sent to the four watcher realms." Adewara picked another book from the pile of brass plates, opened it, and turned to specific pages.

"Here, the inscriptions on the plates read of Ishtar and Obatala wanting access to their technology. Kainoa and Kaimana agreed to share all their technology with Andalusia. Kainoa and Kaimana then agreed to evenly divide their ancient Kemetic bloodlines into four family lines. The divines sent Ninqi and every male of the ancient Nephilim bloodline to Nier's realm. Then they sent Enqi and every male of the ancient Negrunde bloodline to the Neros's realm. Afterward they sent Enil and every male of the ancient Negraté bloodline to the Nethal's realm. Lastly, they sent Sekhmet and every male of the ancient Egyptian bloodline to the Naharis's realm."

"So, with the ancient Kemetic tribes full of men, and the four watcher realms all made of women, what happened next?" Aamira asked as she folded her arms.

"Twelve bloodlines were formed," Adewara replied. "The Orishan bloodline when Nephilim and the Negralli merged. The Yoruban bloodline when the Negrunde and the Anunnaki merged. The Hausan bloodline was formed when the Negraté and the Elohim merged. Lastly, the Demirrian bloodline was formed when the Nelioan's merged their bloodlines with the Egyptians. The other three bloodlines were the Amun bloodline, Aethiopian bloodline, Solar bloodlines, and the Lemba bloodline. These Chosen were made from the twelve bloodlines with the assistance of Ibeji, the nephew and niece of Obatala and Ishtar, ensuring that the Kemetic bloodline stayed concealed within the female at all times."

"According to realm law the merging was forbidden," King Abioye said.

"How is it possible that what they did was against realm law?" Aamira asked.

Abioye tapped his finger against the plates. "If they broke

realm laws, then each realm had the right to fight the other realms. But because all four realms took part in breaking realm law, there was no need for each of them to fight one another."

"You infer incorrectly," Adewara said. "The realm laws were created after eight of the twelve bloodlines merged into four bloodlines. And there was never peace among them; not fully. Distrust was common. We were divided even then, making Natas' plan all the more effective. We will continue to be slaves until we put aside our petty squabbles and worthless pride."

"This is why I must get to Sahael," Aamira said, slamming her hands on the table.

"To find a way into Sahael, we need to learn answers here in the library walls that the quakes knocked down," Adewara said.

Abioye put his arm around his wife's shoulder. "We're in this together now. It's not just you, it's us." He looked at Adewara. "Still, if the entire Alkebulan continent is poisonous and deadly, what do we do to combat that?"

Aamira nodded her head in agreement. You have a lot of knowledge, Adewara. Before we delve into these records, I still have questions you may be able to answer. What happened to the four bloodlines after they merged? What happened afterward in Katunkumene?"

"I'll tell you what I know from the records in Timbuktu," Adewara said. "My knowledge is vast, but I haven't studied everything." He smiled. "I'm older than I look, after all. Still, I'll give you the answers I can. Lord Commander Natas objected to helping the ancient Kemites, which led to the civil war in Katunkumene. As I've told you, this rebellion led to Natas and one-third of the people in Andalusia following him, to fight an unwinnable war. After centuries of battle, both physical and of words, Natas was finally defeated and cast into the realm's outer darkness, the Nothing, for all eternity. After nearly losing to Lord

Commander Natas, Ishtar and Obatala asked Kainoa and Kaimana to help protect them from another attack."

Adewara handed Aamira the metal plates in front of him. "Read the emerald words," Adewara said. "This record contains much of what I'm telling you. Some symbols are difficult to discern, but you'll figure them out, I'm sure."

Aamira grabbed the book and started reading out loud.

"Ishtar and Obatala used the technology of the Kemites by giving Kainoa and Kaimana a seat on the council. In return, they then ordered the Kemites Nebiriau, Nzingha, and Njiru to help create a way for the people in Aarde to protect Sahael, Egyptus, Horn, and Alkebulan. Afterward, they gave another set of seats on the council to every Ancient Kemite, who became their brightest and smarter minds."

Aamira paused, unfamiliar with one of the symbols, before understanding its context by the words around it. "Their names were Nairo, Nullify, Nebuchadnezzar, Necrosis, Neolithic, Nabopollassar, Nááthé, and NeRu; and many others who all helped make Katunkumene impenetrable and Aarde safe. Nairo created all the Nairohenge gates throughout Aarde. The Nairohenge Gates allowed the Kemites the ability to travel to other realms. Nullify created singular gate doors located in Nier's realm, Neros's realm, Nethal's realm, Naharis's realm, Sahael, and possibly Egyptus and Horn as well.

"Nullify's Gates allowed the leaders of Katunkumene to travel to, and from, any of the four realms except for and through Nullify's gate in Naharis's realm. It was connected to the realms of outer darkness," Queen Aamira read. "This next symbol is hard to…I think it's Nebuchadnezzar?"

"Keep reading. You're doing a great job," Adewara said.

"Nebuchadnezzar created portals on each of the four gates

in each of the four realms. They allowed those traveling from Katunkumene the power to move through Nabopollassar's seal and Nullify's gates without being killed and ripped to shreds."

"Ripped to shreds?" Abioye interrupted. "Is that accurate? Is that what will happen if you don't get the gate incantations right?"

"It's not about the incantations," Adewara answered. "But that is why you need Medjay Guardians who know what they're doing. So many are lost or killed. An entire generation of sentinels will need to be trained if we are to reestablish Sahael and a better world." He motioned toward Aamira. "Please, continue."

Aamira nodded, turning a brass page. "Nabopollassar, created multiple seals; one in Nier's Realm was a sapphire seal that allowed magic to flow through it effortlessly. The second seal was an emerald seal in Neros's realm that allowed the spirit energy to flow through it effortlessly. The third seal was a Hematite gray-colored seal in Nethal's realm that allowed life energy to flow through it effortlessly. The fourth seal was Turquoise and allowed Death energy to flow through it effortlessly. These four seals were placed on Nullify's gate in Naharis's realm, a sapphire, emerald, hematite gray, turquoise, and obsidian seals to prevent unwanted entry into Aarde; from the other realms of Darkness although there were eight seals total." She looked up from the thin metal page. "They certainly like the word 'effortlessly,' don't they?"

"It's scripture." Abioye said, swatting his wife's arm playfully.

"Whatever," Aamira shrugged. "Where was I? Oh yes. To ensure that Naharis's realm remained safe, Njiru created eight Kemetic keys, a sapphire key, an emerald key, a diamond key, an obsidian key, and a turquoise key. Njiru placed the sapphire key in Nier's realm, placed the emerald key in Neros's realm, then placed the hematite key in Nethal's realm, and lastly, placed the obsidian inside of Khartoum palace. As a fail-safe, NeRu created their Iris and placed it on all six of Nullify's gates in Aarde; with NeRu's iris closed, each realm could reject anyone from entering with or without their approval or consent."

"You read that Nabopollassar created eight seals, from what you have read, that is seven seals," Abioye said

"Interesting," Adewara said.

"What about the eight seals?" Aamira asked.

"Wait, I have more questions about this," Abioye replied. His brow furrowed. "Then you read that Njiru created five keys; you only read about four keys. What about the fifth key? What about NeRu's sixth iris? From what you read, it mentions that there were six irises, but the book only mentions four of them. And why so many keys and gates and all of that? It seems like there's a lot of needless ritual here."

"Ritual has its place, King Abioye," Adewara said. "Ritual is a form of remembrance, and you also need to remember that these were divided peoples and families. They weren't battling each other but there wasn't unity either. Every people needed their own gates, keys, and so forth. As for the rest? I'm glad you were paying attention enough to see the discrepancies, but you are not privy to that type of information yet and will have to wait to get to Sahael to find out the answers to your questions."

"But you know the answers?" Aamira asked.

"Some of them, yes."

Aamira felt her blood pressure rising "Why not tell us then? Isn't this information we need?"

"Yes," Adewara nodded slowly. "But knowledge given before a person is ready is knowledge with no value. Be patient."

Adewara then handed King Abioye another book of plates.

"Why don't you read from this section, King Abioye. We'll see if my years of tutelage to you were as effective as the mere months I spent with Aamira."

Abioye snorted and opened the book. He glanced over some of the words before starting to read.

"After Kainoa and Kaimana shared their technology with Ishtar and Obatala and the Katunkumene people, Ishtar and Obatala presented their plan once again to two-thirds of the Andalusian people. They presented their second-born son Horus to be the redeemer of the people. They told the population that when all of them were sent down to Aarde, they would have no recollection of their premortal existence. Ishtar and Obatala told them that not all of them would return because they would be allowed to exercise free will."

"That's the plan Natas had fought against," Aamira interrupted.

"Exactly," Adewara confirmed. "Keep reading, Abioye."

"Obatala and Ishtar told them that they would fail since they were no longer perfect beings with perfect knowledge. Ishtar used a veil made to cover their eyes, making them forget as they entered their physical tabernacles, learning everything from the first all over again. After Ishtar finished speaking with them, they all walked through the four lands in Katunkumene, the chosen lands, the Kemet lands, the Nairobi lands, and lastly, the Neru Lands. They entered all four of Nullify's gates being born in Aarde."

After Abioye finished reading, Aamira felt sweat on her body. Having all of this laid out before her, not as a theory or some belief from an enslaved woman singing about redemption, but as fact, as history, she grew angry.

"None of this seems fair," she said.

"What do you mean?" Adewara asked, leaning against the table.

Aamira started pacing. "We come down to Aarde, have no memory of anything, and we're left to suffer at the hands of evil people? That's garbage. That's a stupid plan!"

"Aamira," Abioye said, but she cut him off before he could continue.

"It's stupid! How many innocent children have been born into slavery? How many women have been raped? And that was all part of the plan? I'm just supposed to accept that? Pain and terror that we have no control over? I refuse. How could Obatala, the God Mother, let her children suffer like this? If I ever see her face, she will have to answer for all of this death and the tears of generations."

Adewara placed his hand on her shoulder. "I understand your anger. I do. But you think of this all wrong. What if those who force others to suffer are the ones who will truly wail as the foundations of Aarde fall? What if the physical suffering of mortality is so infinitesimally small compared to an eternity of knowing you failed in your call to uplift your fellow spirits? You have a lot of anger, Aamira. I understand. But your perspective is limited. Just like when you were in that cell for those two months. All you saw was the fact that I and Abioye didn't come to see you, and thus we were horrible people, right?"

"I did think that, yes," Aamira whispered.

"And yet, what you hadn't seen, was the work we were both doing to not only get you out, but to turn the people to your side. The work your new husband did, and the threats he faced, were unknown to you until after. Such is life. We must trust that Ishtar and Obatala have a greater understanding than we do. Their perspective is that of someone standing on the top of a mountain. Ours is that of someone in a crevasse with but a small sliver of sky visible above. Don't lose hope, Aamira. You both must find a way to Sahael if you want answers."

Aamira looked down at the metal book and the aged papers strewn across the table. "How do we do any of this? How do we trust when we feel so much hate toward even our immortal parents?"

A hand touches Aamira's cheek. Adewara smiled. "Trust me for now. Trust your husband. That will be enough."

"…Okay," Aamira said after a pause. She looked at Abioye and smiled slowly.

"Now, if we're talking about getting the two of you to Sahael," Adewara continued. "You have to figure out a way to get there without exposing the people in Karnak to the Narsans, while also preventing General Scipio's armies from wiping them out. We were brought here to the hidden city for a reason. Somewhere hidden in Karnak are the means that could get you to other realms in Aarde."

"Then let's begin," Aamira said, rubbing her palms together.

"It will take years to get through every single book in the library," Adewara smiled. "As an Educator, trust me when I say the answers will not be easy to find, and will require the mixing of pages from different tomes. I will be as much a student here as either of you. I must tell you that time is on our side though, so take all of it you need."

CHAPTER VI
BRANCHES OF THE MARULA TREE

Karnak, The Desert Sand Land of IFF

"I have great news," Aamira said as she walked onto the balcony of their royal quarters. Abioye sat on a stone bench overlooking Karnak with an old book in his hands. The morning sun shone brightly in a cloudless sky.

"What's the news?" Abioye asked. He yawned and closed the book.

"By the blessings of Ibeji, we're expecting," Aamira smiled, touching her stomach.

Abioye shot to his feet and rushed up to his wife, embracing her. "How do you know?"

"Ibeji, visited me three times in the night as I slept, revealing that I'm carrying three of your sons," Aamira laughed.

Abioye's face went blank. "Three?"

Laughter filled the balcony as they hugged and kissed each other.

It had been five months since their wedding. Aamira had expected to get pregnant sooner, but no matter how hard they had tried (and they had tried pretty hard), no pregnancy blessed their union.

Now, their patience had paid off.

"This is great news!" Abioye gushed. "We need to let everyone in Karnak know and celebrate."

Time seemed to flow quickly, like a river that unexpectedly topples over a cataract.

Over the next few months, Adewara continued his research, always telling Aamira he was getting close to finding some answers that could help get them out of Karnak safely. The influx of refugees had stopped, but witan armies continued to search the desert. The main gates to Karnak had magically sealed themselves, allowing no one else to enter or leave. Only by the blessings of Ishtar and Obatala did Karnak remain unfound. During the hottest months of summer, Hashashin spies would return to the city with word that General Scipio's forces had retreated from their search to resupply. The spies would find dead witan soldiers on the dunes; men who had died of dehydration during their hunt for Karnak.

The birth of Aamira and Abioye's children was a welcome sign to all in Karnak. They were healthy and strong, like their parents. The King and Queen named the triplets Yomí, Yekú, and Yemí.

For Aamira, the next ten years passed as though only a few days. She had become accustomed to being queen, and her relationship with Abioye's mother, Adana, had improved since the birth of the boys, though only slightly. Karnak remained peaceful, despite the earthquakes that continued to rumble underfoot regularly. Each prince had their own style and flair to them that distinguished them from each other. Their confidence and aggressive hair styles made them beloved and appreciated by the people.

Much of the decade had been spent learning in the library and underground pyramid complex in the center of Karnak; not just for Aamira and Abioye, but the boys as well. As they grew, the princes learned about their heritage, history, and culture. Prince Yomí, Prince Yekú, and Prince Yemí sat at the feet of their professor, Adewara. He took the boys through the rigid Timbuktu University educational procedures. Even though they were only ten years old, their minds were sharp and inquisitive.

"Are there any more questions?" Adewara asked as King and Queen Adesola, Yomí, Yekú, and Yemí listened to his lecture on the Yoruban bloodline. They sat in the pyramid central room, with angled ceilings one hundred feet above their heads. The boys snacked on dried fruits and honey as they raised their hands to question their instructor.

"Can you tell us more about this place and why we can't leave?" Yomí asked.

"Yeah, like why the Ukáváál wanted this place?" Yekú asked.

"And also, why did the Egyptians build a city Karnak on top of this ancient pyramid?" Yemí asked.

Adewara grinned, always happy to indulge their curiosity.

"That's a lot of questions for the end of a lecture," Adewara said. "If it's alright with the King and Queen, we can stay longer and discuss."

Nodding her head, Aamira waved for Adewara to continue. She loved nothing more than watching her sons get excited over their studies. If only they cared this much about their geometry classes.

The boys quickly gathered around Adewara.

"Yomí, you asked why we couldn't leave this place?" Adewara said, repeating the prince's question.

Yomí nodded his head in confirmation.

"When your mother opened the gates to save the Yoruban people, the entrance was closed preventing the people from leaving this self-sustained oasis. Groups of refugees arrived later and were let in as needed, but once the city was filled, the gates sealed. Staying here is the price for saving the sacred bloodline and preserving a people in despair. That's why this place was built; to keep the sacred bloodline safe. Now, there is one secret path that the Hashashin spies have found through the canyons, but it is difficult and only passable by one person at a time. It would literally take years to get everyone out through that small tunnel. Plus, once they were outside, the armies of Scipio, which still run the desert in force, would easily sweep them away."

Yomí sat forward excitedly. "That's how the Hashashin are able to report to Mom and Dad about the movements of the witan armies in the desert."

Adewara rubbed his hands together. "Yes, that is correct. In order for the people to leave Karnak, the time must be right, and your parents must lead us out toward Sahael."

"What about the Ukáváál?" Yekú asked.

"The Ukáváál wanted this place to establish as a base of operations to begin a campaign of conquest of erasure in Aarde," Adewara explained. "A battle ensued in which the Egyptians battled for years against the Ukáváál, forcing them to the Cendant lands on the other side Aarde."

"Who are these Ukáváál?" Yemí asked. "I've read about them in our studies, but it says only they are a scourge to all life."

A breath blew through Adewara's nostrils. "Not many people know of the Ukáváál. It is deep knowledge. Even many Educators like myself know very little, and even fewer know they exist here on Aarde. The Ukáváál are a race of sentient beings who want to erase people from existence. They are anti-life; mechanical and undead beings who destroyed our original home in the stars. I pray their numbers never grow, and that they remain isolated."

With the mood somber, the boys seemed to be satisfied and asked no more questions.

"That's enough for today, boys," Abioye said as he stood up. "It's time to meet your mother in the training room for your final trials."

"I will meet the three of you shortly," Aamira said as the kids ran past her into the hallway.

Abioye put his arm around Aamira's waist as they watched the boys laughing with other children.

"The boys seem very curious about Ukáváál," he said. "Luckily for them, and for us, the creatures are dormant and no longer a threat."

Adewara grabbed several books from a nearby table and walked up to the royal couple. "Indeed, but that's a conversation for another day."

"But Yomí made a good point," Aamira replied. "We need to find a way out of here. The longer we stay, the more dependent we all become on isolation and the less prepared we'll be for the real word."

"It's a scary thing to think about," Abioye said as his eyes remained focused on their kids, now far down the pyramid hallway. "Our sons' Black skin makes them a threat to all witans, who would rather see them in chains, trafficked, or in some coliseum for their own entertainment. Yet, I understand they need to face and gain these experiences no matter how painful it will be for my heart."

"That should be our focus," Adewara agreed, "looking for a way out of this place for all the people and then we worry about getting to Sahael. Once the gate closed, I knew it would seal for a time, but at this point it's been far longer than I assumed. I believe I've found a handful of answers over the past few months, but putting them together has taken time, and I need your minds and puzzle solving strengths as well. Please follow me."

King and Queen Adesola followed Adewara to the bottom of the pyramid down several deep staircases carved in stone. Torches burned along the walls, giving them their only light. They arrived in a chamber with low ceilings that looked like a mere storage area for grain, but one wall seemed to have broken open onto a tunnel that led into the dark.

"The Emerald guard have cleaned up all of the rubble after a quake last month," Adewara said. "An opening was revealed."

"This tunnel must lead somewhere," Queen Adesola

Adewara ran his finger over a series of carvings in the rock. "This is a Nibiru tunnel. No one realized it was here because they couldn't read the markings on the wall. This room had been used for storage and nothing more. These tunnels were built to conceal the movement of the Kemites, enabling them to travel all over Aarde. They did this to avoid the sunlight that accelerated their life span and made them age more quickly. The Nibiru tunnels had two functions, allowing them to travel and appear at certain points above land anywhere Nibiru hole covers were built."

"This is a way we can get the people out of Karnak and

avoid a slaughter," Abioye said.

"It certainly can," Aamira agreed. "But where does it go? And how long is it?"

"Follow me," Adewara said.

They walked into the darkness, but only about 20 feet, when they came to a stone barrier made of polished obsidian. Aamira walked up to the Nibiru seal and saw the symbol of the Marula Tree and the letter N in the center of the base of the tree.

"It's like the gate that allowed us to enter Karnak over ten and a half years ago," Aamira whispered.

"Exactly," Adewara confirmed. "And as you'll recognize, it has a Nibiru seal on it."

"Didn't the gate of Karnak light up when you touched it, Aamira?" Abioye asked.

She remembered. Her link to these artifacts was undeniable. They had been prepared for her bloodline centuries ago.

Touching her finger against the smooth dark stone, a shiver shot through Aamira's body like electricity. The symbols on the door lit up, activating Aamira's eyes, along with Njiru's rings on her and Abioye's ring fingers, and Nebiriau's bracelet around the queen's wrist.

The tunnel filled with a green glow from the door and Aamira's tattoos. The ground shook, but not with the force of an earthquake; rather a calm vibration that whispered to the mind everything was as it should be. Peace washed over Aamira, and by the look on Abioye and Adewara's faces, they felt the same reassurance.

"Something's happening," Abioye said. "Look!"

The Nibiru wall suddenly became transparent, allowing

entry into the tunnel. The walls themselves glowed with an eternal light, illuminating the chamber as if by the midday sun.

Adewara laughed as a tear rolled down his cheek. "I never thought I would live to set foot in one of these tunnels. The lights on the walls will guide wherever the seeker wishes to go…or at least as close as the hidden entrances will allow. This is a blessed day for all Alkebulans, and all residents of Karnak who have prayed to freely travel again after ten years hidden in these sacred sands."

Footsteps and voices drew Aamira's attention back to the mouth of the tunnel entrance. A group of people had entered the storage chamber.

"Who's down there?" a woman's voice called. It was former Queen Adana. "What's going on?"

"It's us, Mother," Abioye called. "We've found the miracle Adewara has been searching for."

"I could feel something happening as I was searching for you in the pyramid library," Adana said as she approached them in the tunnel. Royal guards stood at the entrance, looking confused in the tunnel's green glow. "Oh my! You've found it! The Nibiru tunnel!" Her fists clenched. "It's a way out of this place and the opportunity to attack General Scipio's army that continues to hunt Karnak."

"No," Adewara said, head shaking. "I would advise against that. We should not be attacking his army now or any time soon. We have the opportunity to sneak away without being detected, allowing the Yorubans people to get away safely and avoid bloodshed."

"What about the opportunity to wipe the desert sand of IFF clean of witan oppression once and for all?" Aamira replied. She and Adana had remained distant over the years, but this was one subject they agreed on. Scipio should pay for the lives he'd taken. They had no way of knowing how many refugees had died over the past decade once the gate sealed itself. How many thousands of Yorubans were slaughtered in the desert because they couldn't enter this sanctuary, all because of Scipio's army?

"I agree with Adewara," Abioye said.

"It's a chance we have to take," Adana continued. "A chance you were willing to take ten years ago, Son. what's changed now?"

"A lot has happened over the years," Abioye answered. "We have children, for one. Rushing in isn't the right thing. Without proper intel, many will die. Remember when Aamira opposed you sending our forces out to face Scipio, and you threw her in the dungeons? That force was destroyed just as she had warned because we weren't properly prepared."

"Isn't that funny?" Adana scoffed with a mirthless smile. "Years ago, we had the upper hand, and I refused to listen to you before a perimeter could be established around Karnak. That sacrifice was worth it because it pushed Scipio off and made him think Karnak was farther north. Sooner or later, they'll find our secret canyon path or stumble upon the city by accident. Karnak will be destroyed, and where do you think they'll look to next? It'll be right here in Cheops Pyramid. It's only a matter of time."

"We will make sure we're gone before that can happen," Abioye said.

"How?" Aamira questioned. She wanted revenge, but the mention of her sons had given her pause. "There's no way to know how close they are to finding us. Our few spies that come and go have never infiltrated Scipio's camp. Plus, we don't know exactly where this tunnel leads. It could take us farther from Sahael, not closer."

"Then a reconnaissance mission will have to be sanctioned to determine where the tunnel goes, and whether or not it is still intact," Abioye said.

Adewara stepped forward, hands pressed together in front of his chest. "If you choose to use the Nibiru tunnels to go above ground, you'll be exposing yourself to uncontrolled actions of others that may force you to do something outside of your control."

"Nevertheless, it's a risk that has to be taken, you know it and I know it," former Queen Adana said.

"Then we need to come up with a sound plan, with contingencies," Abioye agreed.

"Then let's discuss it in the council room," Aamira said.

As they left the tunnel, conflicting emotions bubbled in Aamira's chest. It had been some time since her rage had manifested. For a time, she thought it was under control. Now however, as the opportunity to kill witan soldiers became more of a reality, light shone brightly on her festering anger.

What would she do? How would it affect her boys?

She had no idea.

Adewara brought up Nephrophida's map in the council chambers overlooking Karnak. The sun was setting, but oppressive heat lingered on the air, nonetheless. Aamira and Abioye sat at the head of the stone council table as the leaders of the different families and militia forces filled the room. Former Queen Adana stood with her husband, Themba, near the back of the chamber. Both looked frustrated to be standing so far from the throne.

"If we use the Nibiru tunnels we can get a better idea of General Scipio's position," Adewara explained to the group, pointing at the map. "We'll know his full numbers and those in reserve he's kept hidden in case of a surprise attack."

Aamira stood. "We know from our current spy network that General Scipio has over 400,000 troops that have boxed us in all four sides, and another 200,000 in reserve. Methrol, captain of our guard, brought me the numbers himself just before we gathered here. The estimates are from their last sweep, 12 days ago."

A collective gasp filled the room.

"That's ten times as many people as what we have here in Karnak," one of the patriarchs from the eastern families said. "With all our men, women, and children we couldn't face a force like that."

"If we attack like former Queen Adana wants, our reserves would be wiped out. Even our Emerald Guard," Aamira admitted. Anger had begun to give way to reality.

"Great," Adana shouted from the back of the room. "If all of you wish to cower here, I'll be in my quarters. When you've come up with a plan, let me know."

She left the room with her personal guards. Themba remained.

"That woman drives me nuts," Aamira whispered to Abioye.

"Easy, that's my mother," Abioye said, though he smiled slightly.

"Let's get back to business," Adewara continued. "We need to find General Scipio's third wave. It's hiding out there in the sands somewhere and our spies have only heard whispers of it. We can't risk revealing ourselves without knowing where that wave is located."

"The quakes are intensifying," a representative from the eastern families of Karnak shouted. "One of the pavilions off the main market street on the east side collapsed three days ago during a tremor. We can't wait to be crushed by the sandstone."

Other council members nodded or gave quiet mumbles of support.

"Karnak is intact," Aamira said, arms wide as if inviting all of them to share her vision. "I want battle as much as anyone. We've suffered being trapped here while others of our people have been slaughtered by the thousands. But it makes no sense to destroy ourselves to sate our thirst for revenge."

"Staying here until we know Scipio's movements is the safe play," Abioye said.

"Agreed," Adewara replied.

Abioye stood beside Aamira and pointed at the map. "We hold off for now. When the third wave reveals itself, we can begin to scout the terrain the moment another quake hits the island."

"In the meantime," Aamira said, "keep the entrance to the tunnel guarded at all times. No one is to go near it without my authority. We can't risk someone rushing through the tunnel out of fear and bringing Scipio's army to our doorstep. Adewara, as soon as you see something, or the spies return, please alert me. The boys are waiting for their final tests, which is now more important than ever if we are to potentially face witan armed forces. Join us as soon as you're able."

"I'll join you shortly," Abioye said as Queen Aamira left the council room.

CHAPTER VII
YORUBAN GIFTS

Karnak, The Desert Sand Land of IFF

Queen Aamira waited for Yomí, Yemí, and Yekú to join her in the training room. The ninety thousand square foot room had been groomed specifically for training purposes and had been filled with trees and all kinds of animals such as pumas, tigers, lions, elephants and every type of rodent. For most of the year it acted as a food preserve where excess water was funneled to keep it green.

"Welcome, please sit down," Queen Aamira said as her sons entered the space, laughing and talking.

Yekú, Yemí, and Yomí sat down, doing as their mother ordered.

"Today is exam day," Aamira continued. "The time has come for you all to master your gifts, consisting of your Abilities, Artes, and Powers. These are powers from the Yoruban bloodline that you boys have all inherited from my side of the family."

"What about father?" Yekú asked.

"Your father can use these gifts through me because of Njiru's ring that he wears around his finger. As far as his own gifts and powers, they have yet to be identified, which is a mystery to him and everyone else."

"Understood Mother," Prince Yekú answered.

Aamira nodded. Her sons were so young, and yet they would need to fight as well as full-grown men. She would not hold back in this moment of testing.

"The first of the three Yoruban gifts," she continued, "are your unlimited abilities. These abilities enable you to communicate with the animals of the forest through interspecies communication. These abilities also provide you with the ability to see and hear through all their eyes no matter where you are in the forest. These abilities are stamina, strength, speed, quickness, and endurance. They make you more powerful than you could ever imagine."

"Is that why you and dad forbade us from wrestling with the other kids?" Yekú asked.

"Duh you idiot. Think!" Yomí teased.

"Shut up!" Yekú said.

Yemí just shook his head annoyingly.

"Let me know when you boys are ready," Aamira said.

"Sorry, Mom," Yekú said.

Aamira motioned for the Emerald guards to bring in several weapon racks consisting of ancient Alkebulan shields, swords, and daggers, even a Dahomean Hwi, a Guduf Sword, a Mandinka Knife Saber, and a Senegal Dagger. There were also all kinds of shields ranging from Bamileke shields down to Zulu shields.

"The second of your Yoruban Gifts are your Artes," Aamira explained. "They give you the ability to conjure any type of weapon as long as you've seen it before."

"Like these weapons here?" Yekú asked.

Queen Aamira nodded her head in response.

"Deaf much?" Yomí said.

"Pay attention!" Aamira snapped. "This isn't a game. You may only be ten years old, but as princess of the royal bloodline, you will be hunted in ways you can't yet comprehend. Today you will be tested on your Artes and your capacity to conjure any weapons of your choosing. I know you've practiced your telepathy, but not as much as I've urged. That will be a weakness I will exploit. The last of your Yoruban Gifts is your powers." Aamira waved her hand at the dirt beneath them. When this chamber was created nine years ago to preserve what remained of our herds, I knew it would be a wonderful training ground for not only myself, but you three as well. The dirt allows you to use the power to use Terrakinesis; the ability to control Aarde and its elements."

Aamira stared at her three of her sons. They seemed uncomfortable and nervous.

Good, she thought. *If we will indeed be leaving the safety of Karnak soon, they need to be ready to defend themselves, no matter how young they are.*

"I will give no quarter unless you give up through submission," Aamira added. "This is a live training event in which we will be using real weapons. The game will end when I am defeated or the three of you give up. Look over the weapons rack, the animals in the forest, and the dirt. Feel them. Touch the life around you."

Prince Yekú, Yemí, and Yomí did as their mother ordered, looking over the forest animals, dirt, and the weapon racks.

"It's time to begin," Queen Aamira said. "The last thing the three of you need to know is how to activate your powers; you activate them by blinking your emerald eyes twice, making them

Zambian, a lighter color of emerald green. When this happens, your eyes and natural tattoos will light up, triggering your Yoruban gifts."

Aamira waited for her sons to make eye contact with her, signifying they understood what she'd just said.

"I have Anklohs for each of you that provide the three of you the ability to conjure up any weapon of your choice." She handed each of them a brass bracelet, nodding for them to put them on their forearms. "If you look closely at your Anklohs, you'll see the eye of Ra that will conjure your weapon. The wings coming out of the Ra's eyes provide balance with the weapon as it is used. The handle represents the Black people and the countries of Sahael, Egyptus, Horn, and Alkebulan. You'll be fighting and defending yourselves for the rest of your lives."

Aamira blinked her eyes twice, making them Zambian. An aura formed around her body acting as a protective barrier.

"You see how it works? The last thing you need to know is when you blink your eyes twice, Ra's symbol will match the Zambian in your eyes."

"Yes," All three of them said simultaneously.

"We start now!" Aamira shouted as a green sword formed in her hand as she lunged at the boys.

The boys hesitated, first trying to jump into the air, but Aamira delivered a concussive blow to the chest of Yekú, and Yemí, while spinning in the air and hitting Yomí's as well, knocking all three of them on the ground.

"What the hell?" Yekú said, rubbing his chest.

"This is our exam," Yemí said, jumping to his feet.

"Mom's not holding back," Yomí agreed. "We better figure something out quick."

Aamira landed in between the boys. "Get up and fight back! Any witan that sees you in this position will take you out in seconds and that's how I'm going to treat you."

Aamira attempted to stomp, kick, and sweep her three boys, but they reacted quickly and avoided her attacks.

"Stay here," Yekú shouted to his brothers. "I'll take on Mom first and end this quickly. Follow my lead!" Yekú blinked his eyes twice, making them Zambian just as his mother had taught.

Yemí, and Yomí did the same. Tattoos and symbols lit up all over their body with a green glow.

"Good," Aamira said. "Now you need to find me."

She darted into the trees, running through the dark forest and forcing her sons to pursue her. She opened her mind and saw through the eyes of rats hiding in the grass. As she did, she felt a prodding, knowing one of her sons was doing the same and trying to push her out of the animal's senses.

Good job boys. Use their eyes to find me.

They were doing well but were still no match for their mother.

Aamira appeared as if out of nowhere as her sons ran below her. She leaped from a tree, knocking Yekú down and striking him in the center of his back. Yekú started kicking and punching but Aamira blocked easily and delivered blows of her own, repeatedly punching her son until he started bleeding from his mouth and passed out cold.

Aamira leapt back into the branches above and out of sight. She watched to see what her remaining sons would do. She tried not to think about the fact that she had just beaten her own son senseless. They had to learn this. They had to! The enemies they were sure to face in the coming months and years would show them no mercy. Yekú was unconscious but still alive. General

Scipio would not have been so kind to the boy.

"We need to do something!" Yemí cried. "Mom's gone crazy! Yekú's down and out. Wait here. I have to save him."

"What about me?" Yomí asked.

"Figure something out!" Yemí said.

Aamira leaped down behind her sons. Yemí turned and conjured a double glaive sword In response, Aamira manifested an Egyptian crescent double glaive bow-staff and immediately sprinted toward Yemí.

Yemí blocked Aamira's attack but the Queen quickly countered, hitting Yemí with a roundhouse kick to the side of his head and knocking him unconscious.

"Yemí!" Yomí screamed.

Aamira turned to him, manifesting a sword in each hand in place of the bow-staff.

Yomí blinked his eyes twice making them Zambian. He waved his arms around his body, using his powers of Terrakinesis. Dirt, wood, and mud flew into the air, swirling to trap Aamira. She jumped into the air and escaped the assault, landing in front of Yomí.

Yomí immediately used his powers to summon Ra and Aten Glaives to fight his mother and go on the offensive.

Dashing toward Aamira, Yomí slid on the floor attempting to take out her legs.

Aamira jumped in the air. The ground shook as she flipped. A tall structure of dirt and rock emerged beneath her, and she landed on it like it was a pedestal made especially for her. Thousands of rocks began shooting at Yomí from the column of dirt. He tried to block them, but pebbles smacked his face and arms. The weapons in his hands dissolved.

Aamira jumped from the dirt structure, delivering a blow to Yomí's chest and knocking him into Yekú and Yemí, who had regained consciousness. She leaped again into the trees, concealing herself so she could see how her children would react and adapt.

"We need to do this together," Yekú said as he wiped blood from his nose. "It's the only way we'll be able to win this battle."

"What do you suggest?" Yemí asked. "She's too fast. And crazy!"

"We need to think of something quick because Mom's going to attack us any second," Yomí said.

Yekú conjured an Aether Glaive.

"Wait!" Yomí said. "Did you all see the Zambian that created a protective coating around her entire body? We have to experience all three of our abilities, Artes, powers, all at the same time. That's how we win."

"We need to communicate at the same time," Yekú said.

"Sounds good," Yomí said.

"We all need to attack at the same time using our Yoruban gifts," Yekú continued. "I'll attack Mother directly, Yemí you attack from the right, and Yomí you attack from the left."

Aamira smiled. They were thinking like warriors. Still, they had said their plan out loud, which once again gave her the advantage. They had much to learn.

She dropped behind them silently, but Yemí turned and saw her.

"She's here!" Yemí shouted. "Get her!"

The three princes charged Aamira using their abilities, Artes, and powers.

Yekú made the animals charge after Aamira, distracting

her. Several pumas swiped at her and she was forced to pivot to keep from being mauled.

Yemí took advantage of the momentary opening, using his Artes to attack Aamira while still dodging the animals.

Yomí used the elements of the ground to his advantage, bringing up a gigantic rock and throwing it at Aamira as he charged. The rock hit their mother, knocking her back.

"If we want to defeat mother, we need to bring that rock column she created down on top of us," Yekú said, speaking telepathically. Aamira could hear it, but knew their enemies wouldn't. *"Yomi, you're the best at moving dirt and stuff. You need to do it."*

"Are you sure?" Yomí asked out loud.

"It's the only way," Yemí said.

"Okay," Yomí said as he charged in, bringing the rock structure down on all four of them. Dust billowed everywhere. Aamira coughed. The animals rushed back into the forest.

Silence filled the training room.

What were the boys playing at? Aamira's motherly urge was to rush in and rescue them, but she knew they had a plan, and she had to let it play out.

After several minutes the rubble that Yomí had brought down on everyone started moving.

Yekú, was the first to emerge, then Yemí, and finally Yomí. Their eyes glowed and the Zambian energy encrusted around their bodies. There wasn't a single scratch on any of them.

They had done it.

No further fighting was necessary.

Clapping echoed through the training room as the dust

cleared. The boys looked around confused.

"Well done," Aamira said. "The three of you did what was necessary."

Abioye and Adewara stepped from the trees near the entrance, both clapping enthusiastically.

"Is the fight over?" Yekú asked. His weapons faded away.

"It's over," Aamira confirmed.

"I thought we needed to fight until you were defeated, or we were," Yomí said.

"The true test," Abioye replied, "was for all three of you to manifest your powers and prove you could fight a superior enemy effectively. There was no way you were ever going to beat your mother. Sorry to break it to you."

"Really?" Yemí said, shoulders slumping. "I thought we were doing pretty well."

Aamira rubbed her son's braided head. "You did, but your skills are no match for mine. Not yet. I've trained daily for ten years. Eventually you will be able to beat me, but not today."

"The boys did well," Adewara spoke, arms now folded. "They were willing to give up their lives to win for the greater good."

"Class is dismissed," Aamira said. "Go clean up and enjoy the rest of the day. Play with your friends and laugh. Go!"

The boys left quickly to bathe and get on with the rest of their day.

Three days later, Aamira quietly entered the council chambers where Adewara and Abioye were speaking. They sat at the stone table eating handfuls of dried nuts. She heard her name mentioned and decided to listen to what the two men were discussing.

"She's grown up," Adewara said as he took a drink from a brass goblet. "In the past, your wife would've charged without thinking about the ramifications. She chose not to fight Scipio's forces and instead wait to guarantee the safety of the people. She truly has become the queen this people need."

Abioye nodded, shewing a few nuts. "Aamira understands when to charge and when to have restraint. I know it's taking every fiber in her body to have to hold back when she'd rather wipe out General Scipio. But she's been queen for a long time now. She won't risk losing more of her people than would be required. And look at how well the boys did on their fight test. She was the perfect instructor. I couldn't have done better."

"True," Adewara agreed. "The boys have progressed wonderfully. Aamira has become truly queenly. She used to rush into situations halfcocked and say things without even thinking of the consequences. Remember when she was locked in the dungeons by your mother."

Aamira had heard enough and decided to make her presence known.

"I remember very well," she said.

Adewara and Abioye jumped in surprise.

"Were you eavesdropping again?" Abioye smiled as his wife kissed his cheek. "We know how that played out with the boys last time."

"Ten-year-olds don't need privacy," Aamira said as she took several nuts and threw them in her mouth.

"My Queen!" a voice shouted from the hallway. Two Emerald Guards entered, green capes flowing behind them. Sweat dripped from their faces.

"Speak, Centurion," Aamira replied.

"Our Hashashin spies have returned. General Scipio has revealed his troops, and they have begun their march. Legions seem to be dug inside of trenches as a tertiary defense."

The second guard stepped forward. "There are also other soldiers hiding near the entrance to Karnak. They have found the slot canyon that leads to the gate. It seems the recent spate of quakes opened the canyon wider and the duns poured in, making the entrance obvious to outsiders. The entire army is now mobilized in all directions."

"That can only mean one thing," Adewara said. "The Order."

"Operation Red Dog has begun," the guard confirmed. "The Hashashin documented the General is going to force the remaining remnants of the people out of the four cities, knowing they'll come to Gore to be massacred."

"We need to act fast," Adewara said.

Abioye stood, knocking over one of the goblets and spilling grape juice onto the table. "We need to get everyone in here at once. Call General Taharqa and Captain Methrol immediately. We can now come up with a defense, attack, and contingency strategy to gain the information necessary."

Adewara looked at Aamira. "You have a decision to make, my Queen. Focus and save the Yoruban people or disrupt Madame Delphine's enslaved trafficking ring by attacking Scipio. As the Princess of Sahael and regent of the Yoruban Bloodline, only you can choose."

"My wife will not disappoint," Abioye said, touching

Aamira's arm.

No matter what decision Aamira made, it had the potential to be wrong. Or maybe neither decision was the right one and both would lead to destruction and despair in one way or another. Free her people and leave the colonies to continue suffering? Lead her people to battle against a far more powerful enemy and most likely see the slaughter of thousands of her subjects needlessly? She would have to pick up the pieces and deal with the fallout regardless of her choice.

"I'm going to have to put a group of people in harm's way no matter what," Aamira said slowly.

"You're going to be faced with the same decision your mother was faced with when she decided to put you on the ships as a little girl," Adewara explained.

Before Aamira could reply, Taharqa, the General of Karnak's military, rushed in past the two guards. His gray beard was speckled with sand and sweat.

"There is an urgent matter," Taharqa said.

"The guards have already told us," Aamira said.

"There is more!" he said, wiping his brow.

"What is it, Taharqa?" King Abioye asked.

"Former Queen Adana has taken a small army of her most trusted soldiers through the Nibiru tunnel to confront and fight General Scipio," Taharqa said.

"What?" Adewara shouted.

"She's doomed us all," Aamira said.

"What about the guards we posted in the tunnel?" Abioye asked.

"They were killed, my King."

Once again uncontrollable rage filled Aamira's veins, but not for Scipio's army or the witan slavers, for damn Queen Adana. That selfish woman! It had been ten years since her husband's death. She had since remarried and no longer controlled the nation, and yet her grief continued to poison her and make her angry all the time.

Aamira understood that anger. She knew the same poisoning would happen to her if she let it.

But she wouldn't let it.

"We need to get to the surface as quickly as possible," Aamira ordered. "Alert the people of Karnak, General. Adana will expose our position, giving Scipio the advantage he's waited ten years to obtain. Our soldiers need to be ready."

"I'll mobilize the army," Taharqa said.

"Go," King Abioye said.

Aamira clenched her fists. She would have chosen to protect the people, not send them into battle merely to satisfy her own lust for revenge.

The choice had now been taken away from her.

War stared them in the face.

CHAPTER VIII
SAVE THE QUEEN

IFF Forest, Gore. The Bay of Karnak

The council quickly convened around the stone table. A sense of worry and dread filled the room.

"According to the Nephrophida's map," Taharqa said as he stood at the head of the gathering, "the cities are all under attack. We need to save the people and get them here safely."

"How do we save millions of people when we are on the verge of abandoning Karnak ourselves?" a regent from the north asked.

"The main gate has been discovered," another family head replied. "Even a clumsy and ineffective military leader would be able to find Karnak in a matter of days after that, even if they can't open the barrier. And we're dealing with Scipio, one of Natas' best military minds."

"We can't save the cities," an older woman shouted, waving a cane over her head. "We have to save ourselves!"

"I have an idea," Queen Aamira said. "There are four cities situated by the three rivers. Scipio is attacking from the sands on the west, not from the water. According to our information, there are hundreds of boats in the bay of Karnak that can be used to travel down those rivers secretly to bring the people here safely through Nibiru's tunnel."

"Do the tunnels lead to the rivers?" the old woman asked.

"Why aren't the people escaping by river themselves?" a man in a turban asked. "If it's a safe route, they should be responsible for their own salvation."

Abioye stood next to Taharqa. "The rivers run directly into Scipio's territory on the north and south. According to the Hashashin spies, our tunnels can be opened less than a mile from each city along the water before anyone would be seen by Scipio's forces. Queen Aamira's plan is solid."

"The people need to be warned if they are to know the river is safe," Adewara said.

"Who should we send?" Aamira asked.

"We can send Taharqa," Abioye said.

"No," Adewara said, head shaking back and forth. "We need him on the battlefield. I need him to travel and save the women, men, and children who have escaped in the IFFIAN forest."

"Then who do we send?" Aamira said.

Adewara looked at the Queen. "We must send you and your sons."

"Are you out of your damn mind?" Aamira shouted. "I've never led a military campaign. And my sons are ten-year-olds! You expect them to battle grown men and kill them?" She looked at Abioye, whose face was grave. "Back me up, Abioye. This is insane."

"Adewara's right," Abioye replied, head dropping slightly. "You are the most powerful of us all, whether military trained or not. And our sons proved just a few days ago that they can handle themselves, 10-year-olds or not. They've passed their trials and are ready."

Aamira blinked several times. The room was completely silent.

Adewara took a deep breath. "I know this is not what you want, but as our queen, and one of the future queens of Sahael, this is your duty. And the duty of your sons. You cannot think of yourself only as a mother. You are Queen, and they are princes. The four of you are the most powerful people in all of Karnak or IFF, or even this section of Aarde. The time has come for you to show it."

Pulse pounding, Aamira looked into the faces of the regents and council members. None of them looked her in the eye. They all knew what was being asked of her.

Her life and her son's lives.

Even if they survived, their lives would not be what they were before. She knew firsthand that taking a life was not something that could be removed from a soul. Her little boys would learn that soon enough. They had grown up here in Karnak safe, well fed, and highly trained, where their peers throughout Aarde had lived in slavery, seeing death and rape every day. She could no longer shelter them from the real world. The time had come for them to join the fight.

And it would all be their selfish grandmother's fault. In that moment, all the resentment and hate she had ever felt for the witan slavers, even Natas himself, transferred to that bitch Adana.

"I don't feel comfortable about this at all," Aamira said. "But as queen, I know it is the right decision. Where will we be going?"

"Reports show that former Queen Adana has disrupted the

enslavement tracking operation on the island," Adewara confirmed. "Forcing General Scipio to divert his forces to the IFFIAN Forest. We can send Yekú to Tzaft, Yemí to Zalm, and Yomí to Mikveh. They will save the people and then travel back down the rivers to the Bay of Karnak. It's the perfect diversion, as Yekú, Yemí, and Yomí travel upriver with the boats, General Scipio will be moving his army to the IFFIAN forest, removing the General's eyes and ears from the river. This ensures that the boys will be safe the entire time as we implement our plan of attack."

Suddenly another alternative flashed in Aamira's mind. Were her sons ready to fight? Admittedly, yes. Should they have to? No. Someone else could be sacrificed and protect everyone; someone who deserved it.

"There's no need to send the princes if you simply allow General Scipio to fight former Queen Adana and her troops," Aamira said calmly. "That will divert his forces well enough."

"But, at what cost?" Abioye asked.

"Former Queen Adana and her army," Aamira said nonchalantly.

"What?" Abioye gasped.

"It's the only way to save the people on the Island," Aamira said. "It's a sound strategy. Adewara would agree, I'm sure. He is a Hashashin Assassin as well as an Educator. He knows when sacrifice is needed."

"By sacrificing my mother?" King Abioye yelled.

Aamira stood tall and stared directly into her husband's eyes. "She is sacrificing all of us! She is sacrificing your wife and children! Her actions put tens of thousands of people at risk and have exposed the entrance to this sacred place. Would you put your ten-year-old sons in harm's way to spare your mother for her own actions?"

Abioye breathed heavily as if the extra air would help him rebuff Aamira's argument.

"I didn't think so!" Aamira continued. Everyone in the room watched her as an uncomfortable silence seemed to swallow every word she spoke. "You've always defended your mother no matter what. I understand in principle, but not this time. She has put herself above this people, including you. We should let her pay the price for that folly."

"But…she's my mother," he said quietly.

"She betrayed us!"

"And what if it isn't death that faces her?" Abioye shouted, matching Aamira's tone for the first time. "What if it's enslavement she faces? What if it's rape and servitude? What do you say to that?"

"I say, better her than my children!"

"She's my mother!"

Adewara stepped forward, hands raised as if to calm the royal couple. "Former Queen Adana and your father, King Ayotunde are not your real parents, they're your adopted parents."

"What?" Abioye questioned. "What are you talking about?"

"You're too young to remember," Adewara said. "And now is not the time to go into it."

"No! You'll tell me now! Your King demands it," King Adesola ordered.

"I answer to a higher power," Adewara replied. "Not to you. My orders are to tell you once your home is in order and you have returned the people to Sahael."

Abioye grimaced and swallowed, but eventually nodded.

"I understand, but what about the people in the city of

Beth-din?" Abioye asked. He avoided looking at Aamira as he changed the subject. "They'll have to travel past Gore. Once word reaches General Scipio, he'll travel to the city as quickly as possible, blocking off the three rivers."

"Then we take over Gore city to ensure Yekú, Yemí, and Yomí are safe along with all the people," Aamira said.

"What of Queen Adana?" Adewara asked.

"She made her choice," Aamira said. "Let's all meet at the Nibiru tunnel."

"Your sons will still need to go to their assignments as planned," Adewara said. "If we are sacrificing Queen Adana, that doesn't mean all will be safe. Do you agree for them to be sent to the planned cities?"

Aamira nodded, confident the fighting would be limited and her boys safe.

"Yes."

Queen Aamira, King Abioye, Adewara and General Taharqa all met at the Nibiru tunnel with Karnak's military. Soldiers filled the hallways leading down to the storage room and tunnel. The people of Karnak were all in attendance at the pyramid entrance, quiet and nervous.

Yekú, Yemí, and Yomí were summoned to join the group and receive their assignments.

"You know what is being asked of you?" Abioye said to his three sons.

"Yes, Father," they stated in unison.

Aamira had to admit, she was surprised. The boys didn't look nervous or scared in the least. They seemed excited and ready to defend the people. They were too young for this! Why had the world fallen apart so much to require children to fight for their lives. When would such days cease?

"You fight well," Aamira said, hugging each of her boys. "You proved yourselves worthy. Remember your experience during the trials. You will triumph over any witan enemy. Just don't get cocky. Trust in Ishtar and Obatala and you will be kept safe. Our prayers will reach the ears of our ancestors. We will see each other again."

Adewara stepped forward and addressed the gathered soldiers. "We only have access to the surface. If you'd like access to all Aarde, you'd have to walk through the Nibiru entrance. From there you'll see an unlit flame. The flame of Naki, once lit, makes this barrier passable, allowing the people to travel in large groups to avoid being seen by witans."

"How is the spark to be lit?" Aamira asked as she looked at the large letter 'N' engraved on the back of the storage area wall.

"The spark was lit the moment you and Abioye joined and became one over ten years ago," Abioye confirmed. "If you look below the unlit flame, you'll see a flame box that is locked. What you'll also see are two handprints on each side of the flame box. If the two of you press the handprints at the same time, they will generate a spark that will light Naki's Emerald flame, burning the Zambian mist. The propeller will then be activated from behind Naki's flame. It will spin, moving the Zambian mist from inside the flame box up through Naki's flame. The Zambian mist will be inhaled by the people, unlocking their sacred lineage hidden deep within their bloodline."

Aamira and Abioye stepped into the tunnel, past the original barrier Aamira had already opened. Green light glowed from the walls as they walked. After one hundred yards, Aamira saw the brass box and the handprints on either side, just as Adewara had said. She and her husband placed their hands in the prints and pressed inward at the same time. A spark shot from flint inside the box and a line on the wall inside a carved crevice took fire. The spark traveled to the center of the unlit flame as if on a candle wick. Moments later, Naki's flame lit up, burning the Zambian mist as it was pushed out of the tunnels throughout all of Cheops pyramid.

"The gate is now clear for the people to travel when the time is right!" Adewara shouted, voice echoing down the tunnel.

Aamira and Abioye excited the Nibiru tunnel. They walked up the steps past the soldiers and emerged from the pyramid to see the crowds of people gather on the steps. The eyes of every person in Karnak were now emerald, green. Their irises were lighter and not as dark as the royal families but emerald, nonetheless. The Yoruban bloodline had awakened in their veins The people were now fully under Queen and King Adesola's command, with Queen Aamira as their leader through the Chosen Right of Election.

"My people!" Aamira shouted.

Cheers echoed through Karnak.

"The time has come for us to sojourn beyond these hidden dunes," she continued. "This journey will be long and dangerous. Even our children may have to fight. I have sent my own ten-year-old sons into the path of death, but I do so with hope in Ishtar and Obatala. I carry that same hope with me for each one of you. Let us look to the future and our home in Sahael! Follow me!"

The rocks themselves seemed to vibrate with the ecstatic roar of her people. They weren't afraid of Scipio's army. They were inspired to return to their homeland.

Aamira and Abioye returned to the tunnel entrance and followed Adewara as he led the first contingent of soldiers into the green light.

"I will act as guide," the Educator said as they followed. "While you may not see them, there are other paths that branch out from this one. Anyone untrained could be lost in the Nibiru tunnel. Such is their blessing to the chosen people, and a curse to those unfamiliar with the way of the gods. I just wish we had a Navigator who could lead us farther into the world. I admit, going past the Iffian shores would be beyond my skill."

They walked for several hours. As far as Aamira was concerned, the tunnel never changed course or turned from the left to the right. Subtly she noticed a slight incline, and then without warning, sunlight blinded her for a moment as they stepped into the warm afternoon sun.

They had arrived in the Bay of Karnak.

A wide river to the east a half mile wide stretched in front of them, lined by palm trees and desert dunes beyond. Dozens of large ships lay docked nearby. A city of sandstone buildings and tile roofs lay less than a mile to the north

"We've arrived at Gore," Adewara said. "It is time for us to split up." He turned to the princes. "You are to take control of the ships and travel to the other cities with your men. Listen to your commanders. They will not lead you astray."

Yekú, Yemí, and Yomí left immediately, waving goodbye to their parents. After a brief battle, the sparsely manned ships were taken by the warriors of Karnak. They headed up the three rivers to save the people, traveling with 2,000 warriors each.

After the skirmish, Adewara said goodbye and set off as well, traveling alongside Yemí in captured ships toward the IFFIAN forest with over 14,000 warriors.

Queen Aamira and King Abioye traveled straight for Gore using the Bay of Karnak as cover to move near the city undetected. 80,000 warriors, the bulk of Karnak's forces, followed them.

"Gore's city gates are heavily fortified," Abioye said.

Aamira stared at the iron doors. They had to get Scipio's

soldiers to come out and fight in the open, otherwise this battle would be over before it started. A powerful reflection bounced off the waters of the river and shined on Gore. Anyone looking out from the parapets or stone walls would be blinded by that reflection. Perhaps on no other day of the year would the conditions be this perfect for an assault on Gore.

The gods smile down on the people of Karnak, Aamira thought. *Our victory is predetermined. I hope.*

"We should send 20,000 of our warriors to meet them in open battle, forcing them out of the city," she said.

"We need to capture Gore," Abioye said.

"And if Scipio's forces remain inside, we can't do that. If we fall or are unable to engage the army, refugees from the other cities will be brought here for slaughter. This is our moment. That 20,00 men will draw out the army, allowing the rest of our forces to get behind them. Right now, the sun is reflecting off the waters of the river, masking our presence. I would bet that if we had arrived yesterday or even this time tomorrow, the sun would not be at the exact right angle to create that blinding reflection. If we act now, we can catch them completely by surprise. In another hour, we won't have that advantage."

Abioye looked to the generals standing beside Aamira. "I support the Queen's plan. Draw them out of the city. This will allow us the ability to attack from behind and take control of Gore before they know what's happening."

The Karnak army did as ordered, meeting Lieutenant Taharqa and 20,000 of his warriors on the open battlefield before the gates. Aamira, Abioye, and their 80,000 stayed hidden in the glare produced by the natural contours of the river and angle of the sun.

Taharqa and his men took out the legion of witan guards in

front of Gore as bells began ringing in the city and the alarm was sounded. Within moments the gates opened. Out streamed at least 60,000 soldiers all wearing the red and black garb of Natas. Another 60,000 wore the blue and red of Scipio. Their flags blew in the wind with the symbol of Commander Godek, one of Scipio's most famous lieutenants. Godek's army cheered and taunted, many shouting about how they would easily wipe out this small, sickly force.

Lieutenant Taharqa ordered his men to retreat. The witan soldiers laughed and roared in pride at the fear they had supposedly put into their enemies.

Scipio's men pursued.

With a rallying cry, Taharqa's men turned and rushed into battle. Commander Godek's men, taken aback, began firing arrows. Using their Orichalcum shields, the Karnak forces repelled the attack easily.

Hand-to-hand combat then began. As it did, Aamira and Abioye led their forces behind the witan army and attacked. Completely caught off-guard, Godek's soldiers began falling like leaves in November. Within a half hour, they had taken out over half of Lieutenant Godek's army, using high powered spears, darts, and arrows.

"Push into the city!" Aamira cried.

More forces awaited inside, but they were no match for Karnak's fighters. Aamira herself killed dozens of soldiers with her Yoruban artes. She would leap into a cluster of warriors and conjure blades that would then cut them down as a group. Her armor was covered in blood. Abioye, for his part, led the legions well, more accustomed to giving orders than contributing to the bloodshed. His armor still shined brightly as the afternoon progressed.

After a few hours, Gore had been captured and only 10,000 soldiers of Lieutenant Godek's survived. They hastily retreated into the IFFIAN forest.

"We need to chase them down as soon as possible, before they regroup and attack Adewara," Aamira ordered Taharqa, who was bandaging a wound on his forearm. "We need to alert the people that they need to head this way, and that it's now safe."

"Understood," General Taharqa said, who immediately ordered a contingent of men to start chasing Godek down into the IFFIAN forest.

Aamira stood on the battlements looking out on the river. The sun no longer reflected off the water and she could see where they had exited the tunnel, and the sandy footsteps left behind by their army as they had approached Gore.

"Thank you, Obatala," she said to herself. "Thank you, Ishtar. I know the battle isn't over but thank you for this first victory."

Footsteps behind her told Aamira that her husband approached.

"We have control of the city," Abioye said as he stepped next to her on the wall. "We need to prepare for the attack by General Scipio that's surely to come."

"Something doesn't feel right," Aamira said.

"What do you mean?" Abioye asked.

"We need to make sure the rivers are secure."

"You're worried about the boys?"

Aamira nodded, staring at the water. "Yes, I'm worried. I planned to wipe out Lieutenant Godek's army, not let 10,000 of his men escape. Now we have to follow them into the forest not knowing the events that could happen outside of our own control."

"You know what this means right?" Abioye asked.

"Yes, I do," Aamira replied. "We'll most likely run into former Queen Adana and what's left of her forces."

"As far as we know, my mother could be dead, forced into trafficking, or something worse," Abioye said.

To save her sons, Aamira just might have to save her mother-in-law. And honestly, the thought of anyone, even someone she didn't like, being forced into slavery, made her angry beyond reason.

"Regardless of her choices, it would seem our fates are now one and the same," Queen Aamira said. "We should alert the men that first thing in the morning we head out."

"Then let's make sure we have a plan," Abioye said. "We divide the army and send 10,000 each up the three rivers to provide any help our sons might need. We'll split what remains, leaving half here to protect the city, and the other half will travel with us southwest through the IFFIAN forest. If Scipio attacks here, our force should hold the city easily so long as they stay behind the walls."

"That makes me feel better," Aamira said. "I'll spread the word."

The following morning, Aamira and Abioye set out with their army and charged quickly toward the forest. As they entered the dense foliage, they blinked their eyes, activating their Yoruban gifts. Aamira could see and hear through the eyes and ears of the animals of the forest.

"I can hear the fighting," King Abioye said.

"It's near," Aamira replied. She felt the fear of the creatures nearby and saw bodies of dead witans under the trees as she gazed through the eyes of a puma. Then she noticed animals gnawing on bodies hanging from trees.

She recognized them as Hashashin assassins.

"There are dead bodies all over the sand ground of Hashashin assassins everywhere," King Abioye said. "I see them. They've been slaughtered and hanged from Marula tree branches."

"You know what happened here?" Aamira said, turning to her husband.

"I do," Abioye nodded. "This is General Scipio's work. He didn't head for Gore like we thought he would. He attacked here in full force."

They led their soldiers through a forest of death. Bodies littered the ground. They hadn't gone far when they came upon a ragged encampment of hastily built tents. Aamira saw Adewara tending to the wounded beside a small fire.

"Adewara!" she shouted, running toward her mentor. "What happened?"

"General Scipio's troops have killed all of former Queen Adana's warriors," Adewara answered as he gave a water skin to one of his men. "Our advanced scouts say the queen and all the females that made up the archery units have been placed in cages. Many died struggling, but others were unable to free themselves and are now captured. Scipio slaughtered all the men. I take it if you're here, that Gore is secure?"

"It is," Aamira replied.

"What of our sons?" Abioye asked.

"They safely made it to the three cities and are on their way back to Gore to wait for everyone until they return," Adewara said.

"What of General Taharqa?" Aamira asked.

"He's fighting General Scipio who has cut him off from getting back to the city of Gore," Adewara said, wiping blood from his sword. "The fighting has been fierce. We retreated to rest but were about to head back in and leave the wounded here. Captain Methrol is dead. I believe your stepfather Themba has been killed as well. Many others lay wounded and dying, waiting to breathe their last."

"We need to help Taharqa," Abioye urged. "If Themba is dead, then my mother is suffering more than we could comprehend, whether captured or not."

"Let's rescue everyone that has been taken by Scipio if we can," Aamira said, manifesting a green sword in her right hand. "No one deserves to live in slavery. We'll need to make sure it makes military sense first though. We don't want to put ourselves in a position to be outflanked."

Aamira and Abioye, along with Adewara, moved their army deeper into the forest. Battle cries soon echoed all around as they stumbled upon more dead bodies among the trees. The forest thinned and sand dunes once again encroached on the wood. They positioned themselves to sneak up from behind General Scipio as he attacked what remained of Adewara's forces, and those of General Taharqa.

Looking through the dense trees, Aamira could see the battle raging. Cries of wounded men pierced the ears as limbs were severed and blood coated the sand.

"We need to split our army," Aamira said to Abioye and Adewara. "Send 40,000 each to move in on General Scipio's forces from the right and left, the few men you have with you still, Adewara, moving down the center right behind General Scipio's back."

"Yes, my Queen," Adewara bowed.

"Look!" Abioye shouted suddenly. To their left, surrounded by soldiers, stood cages on wheels being trudged toward the forest by groups of dark-skinned slaves in rags. Inside the cages were women; mainly the archer units from the Karnak army, wearing their green and gold breastplates. In a cage all alone near the front sat former Queen Adana, moaning and whimpering, blood smeared across her chin.

"It's my mother," Abioye cried, stepping forward as if to rush the cages. "She's cold and all alone. We have to save her!"

"I don't think that's a good idea," Aamira replied. "We need to stick to the plan. Scipio's army is right here, vulnerable. We can rescue the prisoners later."

"This is our chance to save her," Abioye urged. "They're coming right for the forest. Please!"

A breath blew from between Aamira's teeth. Her husband's need to please his mother had been a grating trait for ten years. Now it bordered on dangerous, particularly since the only reason they were out here was because of her foolishness and pride. Still, it could present a good opportunity to rescue Karnak's Female Archer Corp that had been ambushed and taken.

"Alright, but she can't return home with us," Aamira said, holding her husband back. "She betrayed our people, and you and I as her rulers. She caused all of this. She will be banished.

"I understand," Abioye said, eyes still fixed on his mother.

As the slaves pulled the cages into the forest, Aamira had the army fall back so they wouldn't be seen. Once the caravan was safely concealed from the battle, they attacked, killing the soldiers acting as escorts and breaking open the cages. The women were overjoyed and quickly ready to rejoin the fight once they had a bit of food and been given new weapons.

Aamira and Abioye personally released Queen Adana from her cage. She looked at them, eyes hollow, face sunken.

"Mother, are you okay?" Abioye asked.

"I'm sorry for what I've done," Adana said, voice scratchy. "But you all need to get out of here. It's a trap!"

"What do you mean?" Aamira questioned, eyes suddenly darting from tree to tree to make sure they weren't being ambushed.

"It's not too late," Adana coughed. "I overheard the Generals talking this morning. This is the same way he killed the Hashashin assassins. They were drawn to save the women in the cages and then they were surrounded and slaughtered."

"Then we need to get out of here before it's too late," King Abioye said.

"My king and queen!" an advanced scout shouted as he ran up to them. "General Scipio and his troops are heading this way! They've turned from Taharqa and are converging on the forest. It looks like another force is moments away from us on the other side to the south too. We're surrounded!"

It was a trap, and they'd fallen right into it.

Aamira shook her head and looked at Adana as Abioye gave her a drink of water from his pouch. Her husband's devotion to his mother had been a strain on them since before their marriage. She hated them both in that moment. They had thrown out all strategy to save one woman. Yes, the archers had been rescued as well, but Aamira knew that if Adana had not been among them, Abioye wouldn't have pushed so hard to rescue them until after the army had been dealt with.

"How long do we have?" Adewara asked the scout.

"Minutes," the soldier replied.

Aamira formed glowing blades in her hands and scanned the forest for movement. She looked at Abioye as he helped his mother stand.

"Get her out of here," she ordered. "Take your mother to the back of the army and return to the camp with the other wounded archers."

Abioye blinked several times before responding, "I need to be here to fight with you."

"You need to be in a place where you'll be of value," Aamira countered. "And that's not here. Your mind isn't on this battle or on me. It's on her. Take the wounded and go."

"Aamira," Abioye said, still holding his mother up.

"We'll talk later," Aamira replied, shaking her head. "Go, before it's too late."

Nodding his head sadly, Abioye led his mother, and the rest of the wounded, back to the dunes on the far side of the forest.

"I'm sorry," Adewara said as he stepped next to Aamira.

"You should be," Aamira said. "This isn't a game we're playing here, and you continue to treat my husband as if he were a ten-year-old. Well, guess where my ten-year-olds are right now. In battle. You're my mentor as much as Abioye's. If he can't be a partner to me over his mother, then I will enter Sahael alone. Do you understand?"

Adewara bowed again. "Yes, my Queen. You speak the truth, and I am truly sorry."

"Be sorry later," Aamira replied, looking away from the retreating group toward what would soon be a wall of enemy soldiers. "Right now, we have to survive, and the only way we can do that is by killing every witan soldier in the sand."

CHAPTER IX
THE WAR FOR IFF

IFF Forest, Gore, The Bay of Karnak

"We need to prepare to fight to the death!" Aamira shouted to the men standing all around in the forest. "Now is not a time for fear, but for action! We can flank them as the lead army enters the forest. I can see their movement as they head this way and then counter the southern army when it arrives. We can reverse our luck by sneaking our warriors past them and making ourselves bait."

"We will need to keep your personal guard with you to draw in General Scipio and then place a small force in the trees as they close in on us," Adewara explained.

"We need to use our advantages as best we can," Aamira said.

Drums rumbled through the trees as Scipio's forces drew closer.

"Let's do it." Aamira opened her mind, seeing through the eyes of the animals in the forest. Most were small mice and the few birds that could survive the heat of IFF in the safety of this small oasis.

"We can distract his military by making the rodents run

across their feet," Aamira said. "The large animals can then charge in, diverting the soldier's eyes away from our moving warriors." She turned to several of the commanders who had gathered around Adewara. "Have your best men climb into the trees now! They can jump from above. We have seconds! Go!"

"We will need to keep your personal guard with you to draw in General Scipio," Adewara said as he pulled a sword from his scabbard.

"Okay, sounds good." Aamira waved her weapon over her head. "Commanders! You heard the plan. Gather your men. We have but moments! Everyone move! You all know what to do."

Through the trees, hundreds of witan soldiers emerged wearing the black and red armor of Natas. Aamira scanned the crowd and caught sight of a tall man surrounded by guards all carrying the flag of Scipio. It had to be the general himself. The man was blond with long hair billowing from beneath a brass helmet. While she could only see a portion of the army through the Marula forest, Aamira knew there still had to be 125,000 soldiers left under Scipio's command according to the most recent reports.

A horn blew, and without any audible order given, Scipio's forces rushed forward. They screamed and cheered as if the battle had already been won.

"Shield wall!" Aamira ordered.

Her personal guard created a shield in a full circle repelling the arrows and swords of General Scipio's soldiers.

"Attack!" she commanded.

Immediately soldiers of Karnak descended from the Marula Trees, ambushing General Scipio's soldiers from above. Hundreds were slashed and killed, but General Scipio's soldiers fired arrows into the Marula Trees, killing many of Aamira's men.

Sending out the command with her mind, Aamira called the

animals to her. Immediately rodents began running through the ranks, disrupting Scipio's line as they shouted and faltered.

The two armies smashed into each other with a ferocity that shocked even Aamira. Like two waves obliterating each other in an ocean storm, the forces slashed and hacked, climbing over bodies to feel their swords against flesh.

"Fight to the death!" Aamira cried.

"Charge!" General Scipio ordered, his voice carrying over the din.

The General's soldiers followed their orders, cutting through Adewara's line and reaching Aamira's personal guard and shield wall.

She manifested an Ankloh and conjured an Egyptian glaive as well.

If she was to die today, Scipio would suffer great losses at her hand.

"Keep your shields up and create an opening allowing General's Scipio's troops in one by one," Aamira ordered.

The guard did as commanded, opening slightly so soldiers could make it through to Aamira one at a time. Each one rushed forward believing they had a chance to kill the princess of Sahael, only to have their head severed from their body before they could even cry out.

The battle raged for another hour, and it became clear Scipio's forces were gaining the advantage. Aamira no longer knew where Adewara was, or if was even alive. General Taharqa was nowhere to be found. Bodies lie everywhere and Aamira would constantly trip on the arms and legs of corpses.

Her own guard began to falter as well, leaving Aamira to fend for herself.

Five soldiers charged her, each covered in the blood of her people.

Aamira darted in their direction, fighting all five of them at once. She blocked their attacks and quickly cut two of them across their stomach, disemboweling them as they fell to the ground.

The following three soldiers came at Aamira from her right, left, and directly in front of her.

Ducking a blow, Aamira swung her curved Ankloh, cutting their legs out from under them.

Adewara rushed over out of nowhere and helped pick her up from the ground.

"We can't keep this up for long," Adewara said. Blood dripped from a wound on his forehead. "Their numbers are overwhelming us."

"We keep fighting! It's the only thing we can do," Aamira replied, taking deep breaths. "Let me connect with the animals and see what is going on."

A rush of images filled Aamira's mind. Many of the animals had been killed by the soldiers, but others watched the battle from the safety of the trees. She saw General Taharqa alive and well, fighting with his men to try and get to Scipio himself, still safe behind his own shield wall.

They needed to buy more time to allow General Taharqa to come up on Scipio from behind.

An idea formed in her mind. A dangerous idea.

"As soon as I move, push forward!" Aamira ordered Adewara. "Take all the men here on the south and fight to the death. Trust me!"

Aamira leapt into the trees just as she had during the final test with her sons. This time she moved directly toward Scipio and his men, no intentions of showing mercy in her mind. She jumped between the two layers of soldiers surrounding the General, catching them off-guard. Within seconds, she had killed four of them, forcing the outer ring to turn around to see what was happening.

And that did it.

The break in the outer line gave Taharqa the advantage he needed. Aamira leapt back into the branches above as Taharqa's men pressed forward, buckling Scipio's line.

"Shield wall!" General Scipio yelled to his troops. "Reform the wall now!"

But the damage had been done. As another wave of rodents disrupted his army, the line was unable to reorganize. His startled and confused men were swept from the field as the army of Karnak swarmed. Aamira jumped from the trees and continually cut holes in the remaining line, sowing chaos throughout the battlefield.

Within an hour, Scipio's troops began crying for mercy.

Adewara and Taharqa led their men forward, swords at the ready, hemming in any retreat. Scipio remained behind his personal guard whose shields remained unbroken.

A hush fell over the forest. The cries of the dying persisted, but the clashing of swords had ceased.

"It's over for you," Aamira shouted, pointing directly at Scipio. "You will die here. You and your troops aren't leaving this island alive."

"Then we will fight to the death," General Scipio called back. "I know you, Sahaelian royal bitch. I serve a greater master than you can possibly imagine; the man who turned your sacred continent of Alkebulan to an uninhabitable wasteland. But I am of import as well, spoken of by the witan prophet Riplakin Denmar two centuries ago in the Book of Remnants. Removing me from this island will result in unimaginable consequences beyond mine or your control. Killing me ushers in the signs of the times, setting the stage for whiteness to take over and spread, starting with the mist that will be carried by the white winds of change. Death will be your enemy as your spirits are ripped away from their bodies."

"What is this you speak of?" Aamira asked.

Adewara touched Aamira's arm. "He speaks of the White Darkness that's to be spread by the white winds."

Aamira had read of such things before but put no stock in witan prophecies. How could such words be real when they were written by rapists and murderers?

She stared at Scipio before spitting on the ground. "Let's finish them off for good!"

"Wise choice," Adewara said.

"Box them in," Aamira ordered.

Her warriors pushed in on General Scipio and his remaining men, cutting them down one by one until only General Scipio remained.

"You think you've won?" Scipio growled.

"It would seem so," Aamira said.

"I will rise once more to haunt you and your loved ones," General Scipio said as he was placed on his knees by Karnak soldiers. His long blond hair blew in the breeze. "You have no idea with whom I and my master are in league. Death is meaningless to us. The more of us die, the more will be raised in glory to eat your flesh and consume your children."

Aamira stepped over multiple dead bodies to get to General Scipio.

"The only thing to be consumed today," she said as she formed a glowing blade in her right hand, "is you by the worms of this forest."

"Then do it, Queen of Karnak; Princess of Sahael; bringer of death to her people," Scipio smiled. "The white winds will soon cover this forest, carrying the white spirits of the Dybbuk into the skies to wait until they are awakened."

With a single swipe, she decapitated General Scipio. His head bounced several feet away, and his body collapsed into a heap.

After a moment's silence, a thick white mist billowed from the ground, wafting on subtle air currents.

"What is this?" Aamira asked.

"The dead bodies are convulsing!" a soldier shouted.

Indeed, the corpses shook and writhed in the mist as if lightning passed through them. The sound of popping joints and chattering teeth sent a chill up Aamira's back.

"It's as if the dead are choking and dying a second time," Adewara yelled.

"There's a white mist coming out of them!" Taharqa cried.

Winds picked up, blowing through the trees until the strange fog dissipated. Aamira looked down at Scipio's dead face, thinking about what he had said. With whom could he and Natas be in league? Who had the power to prophesy what he had spoken and what she had just seen with her own eyes. What were the Dybbuk?

The bodies stopped moving and silence returned. No one moved. Even the bravest soldiers seemed cowered by the jittering dead even after they ceased flinching.

A strange song seemed to fill the forest as if a choir sang somewhere far away.

"I hear something," Aamira said.

"What is it?" Taharqa asked.

"Nova's song," Adewara answered. "The dead are singing the song of retrieval; they want to be found."

Aamira stepped over the bodies to stand next to Adewara. "I thought the song hadn't been heard by non-Demirrians in centuries. That was what the books in the library always said."

"The signs of the times are upon us," Adewara said, looking up at the branches overhead as if staring at the sky. "According to my studies, the Demirrians are responsible for retrieving the bodies of the dead, retuning them to their homelands and burying them. They alone are the ones who can hear Nova's song. That sacred bond between the cursed bloodlines has been severed." He looked at Aamira with a fear she had never seen on his face before. "We need to get to Sahael to find out what's happening. Scipio spoke the truth. Whatever prophecy he referenced; it was delivered by the hand of some knowledgeable deity."

A flash of light to their left drew Aamira's attention. A circle of yellow and purple energy appeared and several men in priestly robes emerged.

"Nebuchadnezzar's Chalcedony portal," Adewara gasped. "Those are Nethanite priests from OutCast Palace."

The priests led wagons being pulled by large lumbering ogres through the portal. Other gateways opened around them, bringing more priests into the forest. They began grabbing corpses by the legs and hefting them into the wagons, all while the air sang around them.

"What's going on?" Aamira asked.

"The Ennead are taking the dead bodies, not the Demirrian," Adewara whispered. "We need to get out of here as soon as possible. As long as we don't engage them, we'll be safe."

"But they're taking the bodies of our soldiers too," Aamira said, forming a blade to stop the priests from taking anyone from Karnak.

"No!" Adewara hissed, grabbing Aamira's arm. "We have to go now. If any of the high priests come through one of those portals and see you, they'll kill you."

"I'd like to see them try!"

"They're powerful!" Adewara confirmed. "We need to go now!"

Aamira accepted Adewara's council and gathered what remained of their army, retreating to the south. Less than fifty percent of their soldiers had survived, but considering they had faced a force more than double their own, the victory was still potent.

Aamira and Adewara sailed through the three rivers the next day, leaving Taharqa with the army. They passed Gore, saluting the lieutenants still in control of the citadel.

By the following afternoon they had returned to Cheops Pyramid in Karnak. There the people rejoiced knowing their Queen had defeated the army of Scipio that had been a constant threat for the past decade. The princes had already returned from their missions in the three cities, and Aamira embraced them.

"They fought well," one of the generals told Aamira, but she was too busy hugging her little ones to pay attention to who had spoken. The boys looked strong and laughed about how they had fought and manipulated the enemy soldiers with their powers just as Aamira had taught them.

They would always be children to her, but now, ten years old or not, they were more men than anyone twice their age.

Pride and relief filled Aamira's heart. They had all been spared. Even so, hundreds of families across Karnak mourned for the loss of husbands, sons, daughters and wives.

At the victory feast that night, Abioye returned without his mother. His eyes were swollen.

"What happened?" Aamira asked as she ate candied fruits that had been prepared for the triumph celebration.

"I told her she couldn't return to Karnak and Cheops Pyramid," Abioye said as he sat next to his wife. "She understood her actions had resulted in her exile. She didn't begrudge you or I."

"Where is she?"

"She summoned her mother and father, King Theseus and Queen Thara of the Minotaur's. She told me they would come from the sacred lands to rescue her. I left her in the desert alone."

He wiped his nose and sniffed.

Aamira felt no compassion for his pains.

The king and queen spoke little to each other during the party. Afterward as they walked back to the royal residence, Abioye asked, "What does all this mean for us? You and me?"

"I don't know," Aamira replied. "I don't know."

They went to bed in silence.

[To be continued on Volume 2 Book 3]